HAWAII EVER AFTER

BURKE BILLIONAIRE ROMANCE BOOK #4

RACHELLE J. CHRISTENSEN

"...A great read for a lazy Sunday afternoon. I highly recommend."

—Diane Darcy, USA Today bestselling author

"Don't expect to get a lot of sleep...If the thrills of the chase don't get you, the thrills of the heart will."

—J. Scott Savage, author of the Mysteries of Cove Series

"*Diamond Rings are Deadly Things* pulled me right in from the first page and held me captive until the very end. Great characters, a compelling plot, a surprising twist at the end... Rachelle Christensen knows how to craft a great mystery."

—*Tristi Pinkston, author of the Secret Sisters Mysteries*

Claire's Christmas Dance

Nonfiction:

What Every 6th Grader Needs to Know: 10 Secrets to Connect Moms & Daughter

Lost Children: Coping with Miscarriage

❀ Created with Vellum

To my readers, thank you for encouraging me to write the next book. I'm so glad that you wanted to know more about Gracie and Pika. I hope you enjoy this story!

And to my Gracie - my beautiful dancer. Thank you for inspiring this character. I love you forever.

CHAPTER ONE

GRACIE

Gracie looked out at the dance floor set up on a grassy area a few hundred yards from the beach. Lexi's Hawaiian wedding had turned out beautifully. Her best friend was stunning in a short cream dress with lace overlay, and she looked blissfully happy. The band played a mixture of traditional wedding music interspersed with Hawaiian style ukuleles. Gracie's toes itched to dance, but instead of feeling joy over this as she had throughout her successful ballet career, tonight she felt depressed.

Mentally shrugging off her gloomy thoughts, Gracie straightened Lexi's veil one last time before Lexi would take the dance floor with her new husband.

"Remember, you're next," Lexi said with a smile.

"Wait, what?" Gracie looked at the bouquet she was holding for Lexi and tried to remember what duty she was forgetting. As the maid of honor for her best friend's

Hawaiian wedding, she'd been busy for the past week helping with last-minute wedding preparations.

"The dance," Lexi whispered. "With Pika."

Gracie's heart jolted at his name, and she forced herself to smile and look at Lexi. "Right. I knew that."

"Relax. You remember Pika."

The music started up, and Gracie nodded toward the dance floor. "You look gorgeous, Mrs. Mitchell. Go have fun."

Gracie did remember Pika, and those memories made her heart hammer in her chest. If she looked across the dance floor and to the left, she would see him. Instead, she focused on the new bride and groom. Lexi and Derek looked so happy and in love as they moved together across the makeshift dance floor, which had been set up underneath the canopy of lush green trees.

Gracie had helped hang white plumeria from the trees on strands of fishing line. The effect in the setting sun was gorgeous. She let out a breath laced with those feelings that had dogged her all the way to the islands—discouragement and disappointment. Her best friend was married, and oh, she was also a billionaire, but Lexi Burke Mitchell didn't act any different toward her college roommate. Most people on the island of Kauai didn't know that she had been part of Burke Enterprises with her brother Jordan.

"I guess it's our turn next," Pika said from her left.

The song was ending, and Gracie had been lost in her thoughts. Pika must have wound his way around the dancing area. She took a shaky breath, turned to him, and smiled. "I almost forgot."

"I didn't," he replied.

Smoldering lava heat rose up from her stomach when she met Pika's eyes. She was totally lying, because she hadn't forgotten any of it either. It had been nine months since she'd visited Lexi and met the handsome Hawaiian native standing in front of her. She'd tried to forget him as she'd lost herself in her ballet career, but his face was the first thing she'd seen every morning since she'd left Hawaii. That face had haunted her through every disappointing audition and subsequent failure and the realization that her life was about to change.

Pika took her hand and guided her toward Lexi and Derek. Everyone clapped as the first dance ended, and they cheered as Derek dipped Lexi and kissed her soundly.

Gracie's heart felt like it was beating in the palm of her hand as Pika interlaced his fingers with hers. He put his other arm around her waist as the next song began, and they swayed to the music. Gracie forgot to be afraid. Pika was a tall, husky Polynesian, and he dwarfed her lithe dancer frame. His dark blue dress shirt was snug across his broad chest, and Gracie wondered if his heart was beating as hard as hers.

"It's really good to see you again," Pika said. "I've wanted to talk to you, but those two have kept us busy." He inclined his head toward Lexi and Derek. "How have you been?"

Gracie hesitated. She'd hoped for this conversation all week, but now that she was in Pika's arms with the perfect opportunity, the old fears kicked in. Pika hadn't called her after she'd left Kauai. She'd justified that action for him, thinking that he probably hadn't expected to see her again.

"I've been working too hard, but I'm planning to be here for a while."

Pika raised his eyebrows. "You are?"

Was that happiness or trepidation in his question? Gracie was overanalyzing everything. *Just dance*, she told herself. *Enjoy this gorgeous guy before he's gone again.* "I'm going to be working with Lexi on some projects here. My last audition didn't pan out."

"I'm sorry to hear that, but at the same time, I'm not sorry," Pika said. "Is that okay for me to say?"

Gracie smiled. "It is. I've had a great career, and things are changing. I need to adapt to the change." If she kept telling herself that, would she believe it one day? The words were a bitter pill to swallow, but they were necessary if she wanted to keep a sunny outlook for the rest of the world.

"It seems things always stay the same here," Pika replied. "Maybe we should do something about that."

With a laugh, Gracie leaned in closer. "Like what?"

Pika pressed his hand on the small of her back. "Hmm, I don't know. Maybe I should take up the hula?"

Gracie snorted. "Not even I could teach you the hula, Pika."

"I don't know about that. Lexi told me how talented you are. I wish I could have seen one of your performances."

Gracie sighed. She wished for that too, because if Pika could see her dance in a ballet performance, it would mean that her career wasn't really over.

"What's that sigh for? Am I that bad of a dancer?" Pika murmured close to her ear.

"No, it's just me resisting change," Gracie replied. She allowed herself to lean into Pika, feeling the hardness of his chest against her cheek. It felt right to be dancing here with Pika. Maybe she needed to stop resisting and accept that there was another path that could bring her happiness. The song wound down, and this was her chance to tell him how she felt. She tilted her head to look up at Pika.

His gaze met hers, and he smiled. "Gracie, I—"

"Pika, sorry to interrupt, but it's Maka." A young boy dressed in cutoff jeans and a T-shirt stood beside them on the dance floor. "They think he might have had a heart attack."

"Ah, not Maka." Pika stepped back from Gracie and then grabbed her hand. "I'm so sorry. I have to go. Please tell Derek and Lexi I'm sorry."

"Okay, but do you need something? Can I help?"

Pika shook his head. "Thank you, but no. Maka is an old friend. It's best if you stay here for Lexi."

He turned and walked swiftly after the young boy, and Gracie wondered if life was playing a cruel trick on her. No more ballet, and a gorgeous Hawaiian who had her heart tangled up in confused knots. Then again, she was here in Kauai instead of freezing in New York City. That's what she would think about. Gracie forced a smile on her face as she walked off the dance floor once again.

CHAPTER TWO

PIKA

"Leilani wants you to take her to the hospital," the young boy said.

"Let's hurry, then," Pika replied.

Pika followed Seti, Leilani's nephew, as he raced to Maka's house. That explained why Leilani hadn't shown up for Derek's wedding—her father, Maka, must have been feeling poorly for most of the day. Pika grunted as he narrowly missed turning his ankle on the uneven back roads that Seti was weaving through. He and Leilani had known each other their whole lives, but they had only started dating seriously three months ago. For the past two months, Pika had been trying to untangle the knots in his heart. He cared for Leilani, but he hadn't experienced the same intensity of feelings that she had—namely feelings that had a wedding hula attached to them.

And now there was Gracie—the ethereal heartbeat that

had flitted in and out of his life last year. The dark-haired, ballet dancer with Italian roots had caught his eye and captured more of his heart than he wanted to admit. In truth, he hadn't thought of Leilani once all evening—not since he'd seen Gracie and felt his heart start pounding out a new, forgotten rhythm.

Seti skidded to a stop in front of the door, hesitating for Pika. "Will Kupuna die?"

Pika put an arm around the boy. Thoughts of Leilani and her father's weak heart felt heavy on his own heart. "I don't think so. He's a fighter."

They opened the door, and Leilani immediately fell into Pika's arms. "Thank you for coming," she sobbed.

Pika held her close and stroked her curly, dark hair. "Maka will be okay. He's had worse before, right?"

Leilani shook her head. "He's older now. I don't know, Pika. I'm not ready for him to go."

"Let's go for a ride. Seti is worried as well." Pika reached out to pat the boy on the head. "Want to come with us?"

Seti nodded and wiped his eyes with his forearm. The poor kid was trying to be strong, while Leilani was falling apart. It worried Pika—maybe things were worse than he'd thought.

Nearly forty minutes later, they arrived at the Kauai Veterans Memorial hospital. They were ushered to a waiting room, where most of Leilani's family was gathered. Her sister, Lenora, jumped up and hugged her son, Seti. "He's going to be okay," she murmured.

"He is?" Leilani asked.

Pika searched the family until his eyes met Leilani's older brother, Brave.

Brave nodded. "His heart is fine. It's a bone spur on his shoulder—caused wicked chest pains, so he thought it was a heart attack."

Pika sank down into a chair with a sigh of relief and a chuckle. "Really? A bone spur?"

"I guess it's somewhat common," Lenora answered. "They're giving him pain relief, and they'll schedule a surgery to get the bone spur removed."

Leilani sat next to Pika and leaned against him. "Thank the heavens."

Pika put his arm around her and nodded. "That is good news."

The family sat and chatted in the waiting room as everyone decompressed from the supposed emergency. Pika felt drained of energy, like an octopus floating in the murky depths of the ocean.

Leilani squeezed his hand and whispered, "I want to get married before anything happens to my parents."

Pika jolted at her words as if he'd been stung by a jelly-fish. "I'm not ready to get married."

Leilani smiled at him and squeezed his hand again. "We should tell my father when we see him. He'll be so happy."

Pika stood abruptly and pulled Leilani up from her chair. "Come with me." He tugged on her hand, leading her outside into the balmy Hawaiian breeze.

"What's the matter?" Leilani asked innocently.

"Leilani, we're not getting married. I haven't asked you to marry me. We're not engaged, and I don't want you saying anything to your father."

Leilani lowered her head and sniffed. "Pika, I love you."

"And I love you, but not in the same way. I'm not ready

for this." Pika waved his hand toward the waiting room bursting with family.

"Maybe you are and you just don't know it. You've known me for forever. How much longer do we wait?"

"Don't push me," Pika nearly growled. She had been pushing him for the past three months, and now that he was standing here, he knew what he had to do. "I have to go. I can't do this anymore."

"I understand." Leilani stepped forward and wrapped her arms around his neck. "It's been a stressful day." She leaned forward onto her tiptoes and covered his mouth with a kiss.

Her lips were soft and familiar. Pika kissed her, but he searched for an ember inside. If he could find one smoldering there, then maybe a spark could ignite his heart and he would feel what Leilani felt. But no. He stepped back. "Please tell your parents of my love."

"Are you sure you have to go?"

"I need some time to figure things out. We need a break. I need some space."

"Sure," she answered with a coy smile. "I'll be waiting for you."

"Leilani, I mean it," Pika said.

Leilani's smile faltered for half a second, but then she nodded. "So do I."

Pika held in his groan as he stomped out to his car. The day hadn't gone at all like he'd planned.

CHAPTER THREE

GRACIE

*H*ow *could paradise feel like a prison?* Gracie thought, and then she immediately felt guilty and ungrateful. Lexi had given her an opportunity to find herself as she retired from professional ballet and searched for the next phase of life. Her joints were constantly inflamed, and after visiting multiple specialists, Gracie had to accept the hard truth: life as she knew it would never be the same. Injuries in her past had caused arthritis, and unless she changed the demands on her body, it would continue to deteriorate. When she had auditioned for the lead role of *Swan Lake*, Gracie knew that if she got the part of Odette, it would be her last full-production ballet. Being passed by for that final opportunity made the bitter pill that much harder to swallow.

Gracie knew plenty of ballerinas who were destroyed once their careers were no longer viable. Drugs, alcohol, and minimum-wage jobs were just some of the horror stories she'd heard and witnessed during the last ten years as she'd watched many friends and acquaintances struggle with the loss of ballet. Dance was her life. It was every serious ballerina's life, and if there were no opportunity to dance— what was life?

Gracie shook her head. That thinking would get her nowhere fast. She took a deep breath and gazed out at the ocean. Those waves were constant and unrelenting. They never gave up, but every single day they changed. The ocean was never the same, and she loved it. Determination to find the ocean in her life swelled within her. Gracie stood and ran toward the shoreline, splashing the water and smiling up at the sun. Yes, it was forced for the moment, but she wasn't a quitter. There was a way to dance through this life; she just needed to learn the steps.

"Gracie? Is that you?"

"Oh!" Gracie shrieked. She whirled around to see Pika standing on the beach. "You scared me!"

"I'm sorry. I didn't know you'd be here, and then I saw you dancing. It was beautiful. I didn't want to interrupt." Pika's eyes were soft. "You're here."

Gracie nodded and took a step toward him. He was gorgeous with his caramel skin and ebony hair that grew in unruly curls approaching his shoulders. She swallowed. What was it he'd said? "I'm here. What are you doing here?"

"Derek gave me a list of things I'm supposed to repair here while they're on their honeymoon." Pika motioned to the sagging deck behind them. "That project is going to take a while."

Gracie put a hand to her forehead. "Oh, I remember now. Lexi mentioned that there would be repairmen around fixing things up, but I didn't know that was you." Wait, that didn't sound right. "I mean, I'm surprised in a good way to see you."

Pika grinned. "So you're staying here for a while?"

Did he seem eager to hear the answer to that question? Gracie mentally scolded herself to stay calm and not get ahead of the dance steps. Pika was a friend. "I'm house-sitting while they are gone. I'm in charge of redecorating the home."

"Really? You decorate too?"

"Lexi tells me I have an eye for interior design, and ... well, how can you go wrong when you have a billionaire footing the redo?"

Pika chuckled. "Fo' sho. But they're the real deal, ya?"

"Yes, Lexi is still the same girl I went to college with. I'm so happy for them." Gracie noted the wistfulness in her tone and cleared her throat. "You must like working with your hands?"

He held up one large brown hand and curled the fingers inward. "It's hard to think of a time when I wasn't holding a machete, a shovel, or a hammer."

And those fine muscles in his arms proved it. His broad shoulders sparked the memory of dancing with him. She'd put her hand on his shoulder and felt the strength underneath. *Stop it, Gracie.* She smiled. "Do you have to rebuild the whole deck?"

"Nah, just parts of it. I'll reinforce and rebuild the railing and replace a good portion of the wood. After that I'll stain it. I'll need to talk to you about color for that, I guess?" Pika walked toward the house and inclined his head to inspect the bottom of the deck.

"Definitely a natural color, nothing too dark. I'm thinking something like this sand." She bent down and picked up a handful of the sticky sand. It was dotted with bits of red, black, and white. Thousands of crushed rocks made up the sand that formed the beautiful beaches of Kauai. She let it filter through her hands and then wiped her hands on her shorts.

"I think that sounds like a good idea. Do you mind if I go inside to get some measurements?"

"Not at all. I'll get you something to drink." Gracie gathered up her beach towel and hat and led the way into the house. Her heart thumped disobediently at Pika's nearness. No matter how many times she told herself to stop, she couldn't resist noticing how he made her feel. "I made a smoothie earlier. Would you like some?"

Pika tilted his head and arched an eyebrow. "Is it one of those green smoothies?"

Gracie smiled and stood on her tiptoes, rolling her shoulders back and raising her arms over her head in a perfect pirouette. "What do you think a dancer would drink?"

With a laugh, Pika nodded. "Okay, I'll try it, but I'm not a huge fan of spinach."

Gracie grabbed the glass bottle from the fridge and poured some for him. "Well, it has spinach, but you can't taste it. I promise." She held out the glass. "It's piña colada."

Pika eyed the light-green drink and then took a swig. He hesitated and then smiled. "Hey, that's delicious."

"Glad you're brave enough to try it." She took a drink,

enjoying the refreshing, healthy mix of sweet pineapple and strawberries. "I used to pack smoothies to take with me after practice. It's a great boost."

"Did you use coconut water in this?"

"And coconut milk."

"No wonder it tastes so good." He finished off his glass in record time and stood there staring as if he was trying to think of what to say.

She stared into his eyes—they were almost black, and his lashes were also black and had a slight curl to them. They were kind eyes, because Pika was kind. He was brawny and muscular, but his smile disarmed her like nothing she'd ever experienced. She leaned toward him, noticing the glow on his sun-kissed skin.

Pika cleared his throat. "Thanks again for the smoothie. I'll get those measurements and get out of your way."

"Oh, I don't mind. It's been pretty quiet here." Why did she say that? Now he would think she was needy.

"I get that. Well, I'll be back tomorrow to make all kinds of ruckus. How about that?"

Gracie smiled. "I think I'd better make a double batch of smoothies."

"I'll bring the fresh coconut." Pika winked, and her insides melted like ice on the hot beach.

He was coming back tomorrow. Her heart was doing the tango and making plans to disobey every rational thought about steering clear of Pika Sepe.

PIKA

*P*ika shouldered a bag of chopped coconuts and another with mangoes, avocados, and a pineapple. He tromped into his grandmother's house.

"Thank you, dear."

"It's my pleasure, my beautiful kupuna."

Grandma chuckled. "It will be your pleasure; of that I'm sure. Just save some for this old wahine."

"Not old, Tutu, just wise." Pika leaned down and pecked his grandma on the cheek. "Maka is doing better today."

Grandma nodded. "Yes, I've been praying for him every hour. And what about your married friends?"

"They're on their honeymoon—someplace in Europe, I think," Pika replied. "They looked happy."

"Good. I like Lexi." Grandma returned to her beads. "Her dark-haired friend was there. What's her name?"

"Gracie Cardulo?" Pika felt an odd flutter in his stomach

when he spoke her name. "Yes, she was the maid of honor. We danced—were dancing when I heard about Maka." There was no way he was going to mention that he'd just come from the house Gracie was staying in.

Grandma made a tsking sound. "Such a lovely young woman. She looked so sad when you left."

"She did?" Pika cast his mind back to the magic of that moment, holding Gracie in his arms. He'd wanted a chance to see her again and had been about to ask before they'd been interrupted. Was it fate that he would now be working in the very house where she was living?

"Will she be on the island for long?" Grandma asked innocently, but Pika knew where the conversation was headed.

"Tutu, don't worry your head or your fingers over women. Leilani is enough trouble for years."

"True."

Gran had never liked Leilani, much to Pika's mother's dismay. Pika had puzzled over the reason, but now he thought he understood. He had ignored dozens of texts and a few calls from Leilani over the past couple days. He didn't want to talk to her, and he definitely didn't want to date her anymore. Leilani didn't awaken his heart. Not the way Gracie did. But he couldn't think about Gracie either. What would a beautiful, talented dancer want with an awkward coconut-chopping brute? "I just need to keep my head down and work."

"Keep your head down but your heart open." Gran reached out and squeezed Pika's fingers.

"I don't even have her number." He didn't mention that

he didn't need her number, since he knew where she lived now *and* would see her tomorrow.

"But Lexi does."

"And she's on her honeymoon."

"Coconuts!" Gran said, and Pika knew that meant it didn't matter.

"Yes, coconuts." He smiled, thinking of the unspoken lecture he'd heard from his grandpa so many times. *"If something is important, don't let anything stand in your way, or you're no different from those coconuts you chop."* Pika grabbed the garbage bag from the kitchen. "I gotta go. I'll take this out with me."

"Thank you, and while you're chopping coconuts, remember what I said."

Pika thought about Gracie as he headed out to the Kalalau Trail to chop coconuts. The timing was right, because a mass of tourists were coming down off the mountain from the beautiful hike. From the Ke'e Beach, a trail rose one thousand feet in a matter of minutes to give onlookers an incredible view of the ocean and parts of the Na Pali coastline. People were usually thirsty and tired by the time they returned from the hike, which could end after a couple miles or turn into a three-day hike. It was the ideal place to chop fresh coconuts, poke in a straw, and sell them.

Derek used to chop coconuts with Pika, but his photography business had flourished, and even if it hadn't, Derek had just married a billionaire. Pika didn't begrudge his friend, but he missed the old times. Life changed, but it wasn't easy to accept the change. Gracie had said something about that as they'd danced. Something about accepting change. Pika had the feeling it meant a change in her dance career. The way Lexi talked, ballet was the only thing Gracie had ever known, and she'd worked harder than most to have an incredibly successful career. Was her career coming to an end? Gracie said she would be staying on Kauai, and even Pika knew that his island wasn't a hub for professional ballets. He swallowed as he thought about what that might mean to Gracie. His heart was calling out to her, and he wanted nothing more than to hold her in his arms right then.

"C'mon, man, the line be long and your mind out in the ocean," Jefe called good-naturedly. His business partner chopped the coconuts rhythmically, never varying his pace.

Pika nodded. "My heart is out there too," he murmured as he chopped the coconuts with renewed vigor.

CHAPTER FIVE

GRACIE

Tuesday morning was more beautiful than the last, which seemed to be the pattern for Hawaii. Gracie bustled around the old house, making a list of everything she needed to do that day. Knowing that Pika was coming today made the whole island look different. Had she really thought it looked like a prison yesterday? She felt a thrill in her stomach. Pika was coming!

She paused and gazed out at the ocean. Yesterday, she'd been feeling sorry for herself before Pika came along. Today, she was positively buzzing with anticipation, yet there was a tiny part of her that warned against getting too excited. Gracie tried to ignore the warning—it was just her old training kicking in, the training to always be perfect. In ballet, perfection was possible, or at least that's what her teachers had drilled into her head. That perfectionism had leaked over into every other area of her life and sucked the fun out of so many things.

Before Lexi's wedding day, Lexi had pulled Gracie aside and made her promise to have fun. "You still think you aren't allowed to have fun, but that's no way to live." Lexi had given her a fierce hug. "Promise me that you will breathe, relax, and for goodness' sake, eat some carbs!"

Gracie smiled as she remembered her best friend's admonition. She stretched in a familiar rhythm that had her almost dancing across the hardwood floors. Her bare feet moved almost of their own volition into a plié and then the first movement. Bits of sand stuck to her feet, and Gracie stopped to examine the floor. The bungalow was nearly thirty years old and had been partially restored in the months since Lexi and Derek had purchased it. The original hardwood flooring had been refinished and sealed, and Gracie appreciated the beautiful dark tones of the mahogany wood against the white walls. Something old and worn had been made beautiful again. Maybe that was part of the reason Lexi had put Gracie in charge of this house: she wanted her to see the potential in something that other people couldn't see.

A knock on the door sent Gracie's insides spinning like hundreds of ballerinas in an ongoing pirouette. Pika. Gracie put a hand to her middle. Just thinking his name had her excited. Oh, why was she even here? She should probably go to the store to buy supplies before she made a fool of herself over the handsome Hawaiian. Even as she thought about the option, her feet moved quickly to the front door. She opened it with a smile.

"Aloha," Pika greeted her with a nod. "Still good for me to work on the deck today?"

At his question, Gracie nodded and tried to figure out how to make her vocal cords work. He looked even better today than he had yesterday. His black hair was thick and wavy, and he brushed it behind his ear as he moved past her into the living room. He walked with confidence and moved like a bear, his heavy footsteps echoing through the room. His thick leg and arm muscles turned Gracie's insides to liquid, and when he turned to her and flashed that brilliant white smile, she felt like her feet were lifting off the ground.

Pika tilted his head. "You doing okay?"

Wait, she still hadn't said anything. Internal facepalm! "Yes, yes, just thinking about the list I've been trying to make for this place. There is still quite a bit to be done."

"That's fo' sho." He motioned toward the deck. "I was really glad to hear that Derek and Lexi wanted to fix this place up."

"Me too," Gracie agreed. "The location is brilliant, and the house has good bones."

Pika tilted his head toward her red suitcase with white polka dots sitting next to the patio door. "Minnie Mouse fan?"

Gracie followed his gaze to the carry-on she hadn't finished unpacking yet. "Yes, longtime fan. I haven't taken the time to unpack everything yet." She loved that he had picked up on the Minnie Mouse theme.

"Hmm, but you are planning to unpack and stay, yeah?"

Gracie grinned. "I am."

"Well, don't let me interrupt your work," Pika said. "I'll just go out here and start making a racket."

Gracie's heart fell, but she made herself nod and answer. "Sure, just let me know if you need anything."

Pika opened the sliding glass door and stepped out onto the deck. It creaked in protest as he dropped his tools. Forcing herself to turn away from Pika was harder than it should have been. Gracie walked into the kitchen and picked up her notebook, continuing the to-do list. The fabric samples she'd ordered should be arriving soon, and then she could get to work ordering throw pillows, rugs, and curtains to match the crisp, clean theme with hints of yellow and red that matched the plumeria growing all over the island.

She jotted down the number of pillows she needed and measured the space for an area rug. When she checked her watch, she saw that she'd been concentrating hard for nearly twelve minutes. Gracie blew out a breath and stole a glance at Pika—it was going to be a long day.

An hour later, Gracie had forced herself to use the computer in the built-in desk in the kitchen to order an area rug and a mat for the front door. She was acutely aware of the banging coming from the deck, but she wouldn't allow herself to stare at Pika's sculpted back, tight beneath his T-shirt as he worked. Okay, she'd stolen a few glances while she was checking the weather.

"Hey, Gracie, can you give me a hand with something?" Pika called.

Gracie jumped so quickly that she banged her knee on the desk. "Oof!" she grunted. "Sure, I'll be right out," she called out as she rubbed her sore knee. Straightening, she walked gingerly toward the deck.

Pika bent down, holding onto a piece of the railing. "If

you wouldn't mind holding this in place, I'll be able to get it straight on the first try."

"Okay." Gracie surveyed the deck. Pika had already ripped out the rotting wood and replaced those sections with new wood—pale in the bright sunlight. "Wow, you're fast."

Pika looked up and smiled at her. "Thanks. You have to work fast this time of year. It could start raining any time."

"I guess we are heading into the rainy season, huh?" Gracie remembered reading something about February being a very wet month for Kauai.

"Yeah, but down here in Poipu, it won't rain near as much as up on the north side near Princeville." He adjusted the beam and looked up at her. "Now hold this steady while I screw the fasteners in."

Gracie did as directed and enjoyed the chance to admire Pika's biceps—they flexed quite nicely when he used the drill and secured the railing.

"So you're really serious about sticking around for a while, yeah?" Pika turned his head to see her face.

"Yes, I have plans to work with Lexi on her foundation." Gracie wished that her voice sounded more confident. It was that part of her that still hadn't completely accepted the new direction of her life—a direction that might take her away from dancing permanently.

"I'm glad. I really wasn't sure that I'd ever see you again," Pika said wistfully.

Gracie swallowed. He *had* thought about her. "I wondered the same thing. It really is good to see your face again."

"The island's not too bad either, right?" Pika powered the drill into action again.

"I love this island, and I'm ready to try some new things." She stepped forward, holding the beam where Pika indicated. He was one of the most beautiful things on the island.

"That's good to hear," Pika said. "Hold this steady, right here." Pika motioned to the next section.

Gracie took in a breath of fresh ocean air. Maybe this new direction wouldn't be so bad. Once Lexi returned from her honeymoon, they could work together on Burke's Higher Steps—the foundation that spanned the globe with goodness. Gracie smiled, thinking of the people Lexi had already helped. The Heart of Atlanta refugee center was just one place that was still in operation because of Lexi. And that story had an especially happy ending for her assistant Shawn.

"How much of the island have you seen?" Pika interrupted her thoughts.

"Not much, but I plan to get to know this island like a native while I'm here," Gracie replied. "I want to know all the best places—not just the places where tourists go."

"Have you ever heard of Stone Dam?"

"No, where is that?"

"It's on the north shore on some private property. Not too many people know about it—at least not many tourists. It's beautiful."

"Is there any place on Kauai that isn't beautiful?" Gracie smirked.

"Hmm, I'll have to get back to ya on that one." He screwed in another board and then leaned back, dusting his hands off. "I wondered if you'd like to go with me? It's an easy hike, and we could take some lunch."

"You want to go with me?" Had he just asked her out? Thoughts of being with Pika on a date collided in her mind with her continual reminder not to fall all over the handsome Hawaiian.

"You busy tomorrow morning?" Pika pushed his curly hair behind his ear and stood.

"No, how early?" Wait, was she sounding too eager? Gracie licked her lips. "I mean, other than a few jobs around here, I should be able to go."

Pika nodded. "I need to put in a few more hours on this deck in the morning, so I'll start by six-thirty, if that's okay."

"Sure. I'm an early riser."

"Good. I think we could fit in the drive and the hike before I hit the base of the Kalalau Trail to chop coconuts." He swung his arm as if he held a machete.

"You've been working there for years, haven't you? It's on the north shore, right?"

"Yeah, and as long as the weather holds, I'm there nearly every day." Pika glanced at the sky. "It can be sunny and dry here and be pouring on the other side of the island. It's easy, consistent money, and I don't mind the work."

Gracie heard something in his answer, almost a hint of defensiveness. Was he self-conscious about his job? "You have a dream job—working right by the ocean every day and enjoying the fresh air. Is that trail hard to hike?"

Pika nodded and his eyes lit up as he smiled. "Mind if I grab a drink?" He motioned inside the house.

"Not at all." She followed him inside the house.

"That trailhead leads to more than one hike." Pika took

a glass from the cupboard and turned on the tap. "People get special permits to go on the full hike—takes about three days and goes along the coast up into the mountain. You have to pack in your own drinking water and gear. Most people just hike partway down to one of the beaches and then turn around and come back."

"Three days?" Gracie's mouth dropped open. "On a hike?"

Pika chuckled and then took a drink of water. "It's amazing. The Na Pali coastline must be the most beautiful place in the world. People come from all over to see it. But the first leg of the hike only takes an hour or two, depending on how far you go."

"You've done the three-day hike?"

"Sure, a few times. I went with my dad when I was a kid. Good times before we lost him to cancer."

"I'm sorry to hear that."

"It was a long time ago, but thanks." Pika set down his glass. "I'd better get back to work so I'll have time to take a pretty lady up to the north shore tomorrow."

Gracie smiled. "I'd better get my work done too, then."

She watched him walk back out to the deck. It was a good thing her workload wasn't overwhelming, because it was difficult to concentrate on fabric and curtains when the landscape in front of her was so distractingly gorgeous.

CHAPTER SIX

PIKA

Chopping coconuts kept Pika busy and engrossed in his thoughts. There wasn't even much time to chitchat with his coworker, Jefe, which was probably good, because Pika didn't want to talk about what was on his mind: Gracie. That wouldn't be expected, because most people had already made plans for him and Leilani to become a permanent fixture on the island. The more time he spent apart from Leilani, the more certain he became that she wasn't good for his heart. He was grateful that he'd broken up with her before it got any more serious.

Pika smiled when he thought of Gracie. Her name suited her, because every movement emanated grace. She was soft, yet strong and alluring. Tomorrow couldn't come soon enough. She had seemed excited when he'd offered to take her to see Stone Dam, and he thought that she liked him. They had hit it off last year, but then the ocean came between them and he didn't attempt to contact the beautiful dancer who seemed out of his league. He was determined not to let this second chance pass him by.

It was after eight and already dark by the time Pika found his way down from the north shore. Princeville was dotted with vacation homes and condominiums. Pika preferred the quiet, rustic neighborhood of Hanapepe he'd been raised in. He stopped by his mother's house, as he did at least three times a week. He often brought Kima the coconuts that they had prepped but hadn't sold. She used them to make the best haupia, and if she was in a good mood, she would make cake with the Hawaiian custard. It was a good excuse to check in on her.

"Still working on frames for Derek?" Pika said as he walked through the door and saw Kima's spread of arts and craft supplies on the kitchen table.

"What do you think of this one?" Kima held up a frame woven from palm leaves and shiny with some sort of lacquer.

"That's nice, and it will probably travel well." He bent and kissed his mother on the cheek. "You're always coming up with something new. Derek's lucky he found you." His mother kept busy with a side gig making frames for Derek to sell with his island photography. His business had taken off, and fortunately, it kept Kima busy as well. The income was a blessing in their lives. Pika just didn't make enough to provide for his mother on his own.

"Pshaw, we both know that you're responsible for my job." Kima patted his cheek. "You're a good son."

"Thanks, Makuahine."

"I know my Pika is a good boy, so I was surprised to see sweet Leilani's tears today."

Pika had headed toward the kitchen to deposit his coconuts. He dropped the bag and swiveled. "What do you mean?"

"Leilani says you've been ignoring her, that you're trying to avoid talking about marriage."

Pika covered his face with his hand and groaned. He should have visited his grandmother instead. So, his talk of breaking up hadn't been as effective as he'd hoped, especially if his ex-girlfriend was recruiting his mother to guilt-trip him. Taking a deep breath, Pika sat down next to Kima. "What she says isn't true."

"I think you need to settle down. It's time for you to quit running from who you're meant to be." Kima focused on her weaving as she spoke. "I thought you loved Leilani."

"Makuahine, I need you to listen to me." He paused, but his mother continued weaving. "Please?"

Kima looked up and studied Pika's face. "What is it?"

"I don't love Leilani like that, and I don't want to marry her. I broke up with her, but it sounds like she didn't accept the truth."

"No." Kima gasped. "You really broke up with her? But she's perfect for you."

Pika put his large hand over his mother's work-worn hand. "No, she isn't perfect for me, and I need you to believe me. I don't want to hurt Leilani, but if you're encouraging her to go after me, she *is* going to get hurt."

"What brought this on, my son?" She put her other hand on top of his. "I just want you to be happy."

"I know, and I am happy. I will find the right girl, but

you have to trust that I know my heart." He tapped his chest.

Kima tsked. "How long must a woman wait for grand-children?"

Pika laughed and stood, careful not to bump Kima's supplies. "I should have known that was the real reason. Why don't I bring you home another friend from stray cat beach?" The beach was the first one tourists came to on the Kalalau Trail, and it was indeed home to several stray cats. Pika had brought one home to his mother a couple years ago, and the cat had loved its new home.

Now Kima laughed, her smile widening and light coming into her eyes. "You'd better not."

"I will if you keep trying to marry me off."

Kima shook her finger at him. "Don't tease your mother. I'm getting old, and I want to see you settle down."

"Okay, I'll do my best." Pika sighed and gave his mother a smile as he walked out the front door.

It wasn't like he was out causing trouble, and he certainly wasn't a womanizer like his cousin Hagan, who had a new girlfriend every week and left a trail of broken hearts in his wake. Pika frowned. Leilani was conniving—he'd give her that. She had no business getting his mother upset. He'd have to do something about her, but he wasn't sure what to do yet. He stifled a groan. He didn't want to think about Leilani. It was Gracie who traced his thoughts and brought a smile to his face. He could figure Leilani Kamai out another day. Tomorrow he was taking Gracie Cardulo on a date, and she would have his complete attention.

He was nearly home when his phone buzzed with an

incoming call, and he frowned when he saw Leilani's face on the screen. He thought about ignoring the call, but then he decided it was best to get this over with.

"Yeah, it's me," Pika said, gripping the phone tightly.

"Pika! I've been so worried. You haven't answered my calls or texts. I haven't seen or heard from you for days!"

"Hey, Leilani. You know the drill. I work, and then I work some more."

"Yes, you work too much. You don't even have time for your girlfriend."

Pika grunted. "You're not my girlfriend, Lei."

"Since when?" she asked with an innocent lilt to her voice.

"Since I broke up with you Friday night. I told you I needed space."

"Space does not equal breaking up with the girl you're about to marry." Leilani sniffed. "Why did you lead me on if you were just going to break my heart?"

"Listen, Leilani," Pika growled. "I am not going to marry you, and I never suggested marriage. That was all you. We were dating, and you took things too far, too fast. We're different, and I see that now. I care for you, but I don't want to date you anymore. I wish you all the best."

"But Pika!" Her voice took on a hysterical pitch. "You can't mean what you're saying. You're just stressed. I'm sorry I didn't give you space. I can do that. I won't call or text. You can have space for your heart to think about us, to think about me."

Pika was about ready to bang his head on the steering wheel as he pulled up to his house. "Please don't make me repeat myself again, Lei. You and I are over. I'm sorry."

"You're just tired. Get some rest. You'll feel better in the morning, and then we can talk. I love you, Pika. You are the only man for me."

Before he could answer, she ended the call. Pika swore as he got out of the car, banging his knee on the door. He barged into his house and flipped on the lights, pushing his hand through his hair. If only he was still chopping coconuts. He could make it through an entire pickup load with the anger coursing through his body.

He banged around his house for twenty minutes, mulling over Leilani's words and tenacity. She wouldn't take no for an answer, but he was done arguing. With a deep breath, he blew out his frustration and decided to concentrate on the one good thing on the horizon—Gracie.

CHAPTER SEVEN

GRACIE

Gracie awoke early to stretch and prepare for her date with Pika. Since he'd be working at the house first, she wanted to be ready, but not seem like she was trying too hard. She chose a pair of lightweight capris in a dark green fabric, and she paired them with a white tank top. Gold hoop earrings and light makeup with a dusting of bronzer completed the look. The weather forecast for the north shore area predicted a light breeze, temperatures around seventy, and a slight chance of rain. Typical for Kauai, and perfect for an outing. Gracie pulled her hair back into a messy bun and smiled at herself in the mirror. She hadn't been this excited for a date in, well, too long. Hopefully, she wasn't building things up too much in her mind. What if Pika didn't feel the same way?

Rolling her shoulders back, Gracie decided to believe

that he noticed the spark between them and was looking forward to the time spent with her as well.

She concentrated on her list again. She didn't want to be waiting at the door like a lost puppy when he showed up. Walking around the house with her notebook in hand, Gracie ticked off the items she needed to concentrate on. Anything to keep her mind off Pika for a few more minutes.

It was just past six-thirty when she heard his truck pulling into the gravel driveway.

Gracie opened the door before he could knock. "Good morning," she said cheerfully.

"It is a good morning. And it looks like the weather is going to cooperate with us today." He carried his bag of tools in with him and walked across the living room. "I'm gonna work as fast as I can so we can leave about nine. Does that sound okay?"

"That sounds perfect. It'll give me motivation to get some of my work done as well."

"I hope you don't mind sandwiches. I picked some up at the market for a little picnic. They're my favorite go-to lunch, and I brought some chocolate-covered macadamia nuts too."

"You're making me hungry already."

Pika stared at her for a moment. "You're definitely making me hungry." He winked, and a giggle escaped before she could stop it. His dark eyebrows lifted slightly. "You have a cute laugh."

"Thanks. Now I'll let you get to work so we can leave on time," Gracie said before he could melt her insides further with his smoldering gaze.

Pika looked out at the deck and then back to her. "I'll be outside."

A few minutes later, Gracie heard him whistling from the deck, and she put a hand over her heart. The sizzle of fireworks from earlier was a low simmer now, but one thing was certain: Pika was irresistible.

PIKA DRILLED in each screw methodically as he replayed the scene from earlier with Gracie. The innocent giggle had burst out of her, and it was almost like it'd caught her by surprise as well. He wondered how long it had been since she'd been away from the grueling pace of a professional ballerina. He didn't know much about ballet other than that ballerinas looked graceful and incredibly flexible, but it seemed the career was more soul-sucking than it appeared on the surface. Gracie reminded him a bit of Lexi when she'd first come to the island from Burke Enterprises in Chicago. It'd taken Lexi a while to find her own pace among the island way of life.

There were plenty of people who tried out the island way and returned to the mainland and the hectic pace they were used to. He hoped Gracie would make it. Pika smiled to himself. He had been openly flirting with her, and he loved the hint of a blush on her cheeks and the way her dark eyes lit up when she laughed. There was a definite contrast between Gracie and Leilani; the eyes were the first key. Although Leilani had beautiful eyes, there was something he had noticed of late that had his heart retreating away from her. There was something cunning and calculating about her. She seemed to always have an agenda, which wasn't too hard to figure out. Her agenda was to get married—to him. Pika shook his head. No use letting thoughts of his ex-girlfriend cloud the day.

A couple of hours later, he stood back to examine his work. The deck had been unstable and dangerous before, but he'd restored it to a state of stability. He still had some work to do on the railing and the expansion off one side that Derek had requested. Once he stained the wood and applied the sealant, it would look a hundred times better than before. He took in a deep breath of the salty, humid air. He loved working outside, loved being near the ocean, loved everything about Hawaii. Today was a day to remember how good life could be. He whistled as he put away his tools and then opened the patio door.

"All finished for today," Pika called out.

"Oh, you startled me," Gracie said as she emerged from the office. "That went by faster than I thought."

"Do you need a little more time to work?"

"No way. Let's get out of here."

Pika chuckled. "I like your enthusiasm. I'll just put my tools in the truck."

"I cut up a pineapple to bring along."

"A girl after my own heart."

And there was that blush again. He liked seeing evidence that she was possibly attracted to him.

Gracie grabbed a pink canvas bag and put it on her shoulder. "I have a couple water bottles too. I'll lock up on our way out."

Pika stowed his tools in the back of the pickup and held the door open for Gracie.

"Thank you," she murmured as he closed the door.

His heart thumped as he walked around to the driver's side. He suddenly felt self-conscious about everything. His red pickup was spotted with rust, but it ran well, and he kept it clean. He was taking this beautiful girl out on a date in between his two jobs. He didn't have his own place and didn't have much in the way of material things. He held back a sigh as he opened the door. What if Gracie was just humoring him because she was lonely? Pika started up the pickup and looked over at her.

"This is going to be so much fun!" She turned to him with her beautiful smile. "And look, clear skies." She pointed toward the blue sky.

Pika chuckled. "For now." He pulled out onto the road; his heart felt a little lighter at Gracie's enthusiasm. She seemed genuinely excited for their date. It was time to quit doubting himself and roll with it.

Gracie lowered her window and took a deep breath. "Don't you love how even the air smells like flowers here?"

"It's how the air should smell, yeah? You mainlanders don't breathe right."

"I guess this is all you've ever known, huh?" Gracie looked out the window. "Do you think I could be happy here?"

"I can't imagine living anywhere else." Pika glanced over at her. "But my kupuna—I mean, my grandpa—he says that you make your own happiness. Some people live in the mountains, some on the beach, some on concrete, but they each can be happy."

"I like that. I guess I'm struggling because I'm not sure what I want to do for a job. I mean, how do you come up with a new career when you've done the same thing your whole life? I love dancing, and I knew that it couldn't last forever, but I wish I had prepared better for the inevitable."

"Would you go back to ballet if you could?"

"I tried out for the lead role in Swan Lake before I moved here. If I got the part, it would have been my last full production ballet." Gracie shrugged. "If there was an opportunity to be part of a short-term production, I might consider it, but my career is over. My body rebelled and started forming arthritis in my joints. The doctor told me that unless things changed, I might not be able to walk by the time I'm sixty."

"Oh, sorry. That sucks major. I'm sorry you didn't get that last role," Pika said, wishing that he hadn't asked. The resignation in Gracie's voice was palpable. He didn't want to dredge up sad thoughts. "Maybe you'll find a part of life that makes you happier than dance?"

Gracie gave him a soft smile. "That's the kind of attitude I need to have. It's been pretty tough accepting that my body can't keep up with me."

"For now, in that one area, right?" Pika replied. "But you can do so many other things. I've seen you move, and you're beautiful."

"Thanks, Pika." She reached a hand over and rested it on his as they drove. He glanced down at her slender fingers and felt a rush of warmth where her skin touched his. It was only a friendly gesture, but it felt like more. He didn't want to admit how much he wanted it to be more.

They continued talking as they drove the winding highway up towards Princeville, and the time passed quickly. It took just over an hour to reach Kahiliholo Road, and the verdant shades of green grew more breathtaking by the minute.

When Pika pulled into the parking area, Gracie gasped. "It's so beautiful."

He chuckled at her exuberance. "We aren't even there yet. Wait until we hike for a bit, and then you'll really be impressed."

They stopped first to sign a waiver to hike the private property. Gracie picked up a map and began reading out loud some of the details Pika was already familiar with.

"It says here that this part of the Kilauea Forest houses the largest mahogany plantation in North America. And the Stone Dam is a historic site built in the 1880s to support the Kilauea sugarcane plantation. Pika, this is going to be so neat to see!" Gracie lifted up onto her tiptoes.

Pika grinned. He felt more alive just being with Gracie.

"Wow, they said it could take us up to four hours to hike." The skin between her eyes puckered with worry.

"Not us," Pika replied with a chuckle. "I've seen you move. It should only take us a little over two hours."

"I have noticed that I don't tire as easily," Gracie said. "I didn't know it would make such a difference being at sea level, but living at a higher elevation coupled with working out for so many years has definitely made my lungs strong. I think you're right. It's going to be a great hike."

They entered the Wai Koa Loop Trail and started off into the forest of tall mahogany trees. Pika reached out his hand, and Gracie took it. He gave her a slight tug, pulling her forward, and Gracie laughed as she bumped into him. "Sorry, I was trying to help you along."

"I know, but I think you forget how strong you are." She tapped his bicep and smiled.

A thrill shot through his stomach at Gracie's innocent touch. "More like I forget how you're light and graceful as a butterfly."

Gracie ducked her head, but not before he caught sight of her bronzed cheeks turning rosy with a blush. She seemed to get more beautiful by the minute. They walked hand in hand for a few moments as the trail slanted slightly upward. When Gracie stopped to investigate a purple-and-white orchid blooming from a tree trunk, Pika admired the way a few curls of her dark hair escaped her bun and flowed over her shoulders.

"Aren't these orchids amazing? I love how fragile, yet wild they look growing on these trees."

"That's a good way to describe them, and another flower I see," he said. She stood and caught him staring at her, and he tilted his head to the side and held out his hands. "You're prettier than any flower, you know."

"Thank you." She fell into step beside him, and they chatted easily about island life as they continued the easy, level hike. They passed a horse farm, and Gracie exclaimed over the animals and the flora and fauna all around them. He already appreciated his island, but it was wonderful to walk beside someone who radiated so much joy. Gracie was a reflection of the sunlight and beauty around them.

When they were within a few hundred yards of the dam, the path plateaued out into a green vista of tough island grasses dotted with purple and pink flowers. Gracie flitted from one plant and flower to the next like an excited butterfly guzzling the nectar of the island. As Pika admired her beauty and exuberance, he began to see the area in a new light. Even though he loved his island, perhaps he took things for granted. It was so refreshing to be around someone who filled him with life instead of draining his soul.

He gave his head a shake. Why had he stayed around Leilani so long? The contrast between the two women was so stark that he felt stupid for not seeing it before. He felt happy today and at peace because he was with Gracie. Even if things didn't progress for them, he had at least learned a valuable lesson. The woman he would give his whole heart to would be one who could cherish it and give back in return.

"Hmm, either you're hungry or that flower is edible."

"What? Huh?" He had been so lost in thought that it appeared he was staring hungrily at a group of orchids trailing down the trunk of tree.

Gracie laughed. "Earth to Pika."

"You're right. I am hungry. Let's eat."

Pika slipped the backpack off his shoulders and pulled out wrapped sandwiches. They sat on the grass and ate heartily. With the addition of Gracie's smoothies, they were satisfied, and he wished for a nap and the chance to curl up with her next to him under the sun.

Gracie leaned back and rolled her shoulders. "I love how lush everything is—so green and alive."

"What other places did you see when you came here to visit before?"

"I went to see Waimea Canyon with Lexi and Derek. I couldn't believe it."

"Yeah, that's the leeward side of the island. That means

that it doesn't get much rain, so there are desert areas and then you drive half an hour and you're in the jungle."

"I never imagined that there could be so much variety on one little island." Gracie inhaled slowly and closed her eyes.

Pika admired her, searching for words that wouldn't just sound like a lame pickup line. He cleared his throat, and she opened her eyes. "It's fun seeing my island through your eyes. I'm glad you appreciate it."

"I want to get to know this island and embrace my new future. I'm not here on vacation, but I don't yet feel like it's home, you know?" Gracie waved her arm toward the waterfall flowing from the dam. "But at the same time, I hope I never quite get used to how nature has made such a masterpiece here."

"The island is always changing." He looked up and noticed clouds moving in, covering the sun. "The weather is somewhat predictable in that it always varies, but yes, the one constant is that it really is paradise." Pika ventured outside of his comfort zone with words and held his breath, wondering how Gracie might react.

She reached for his hand and squeezed it. "Thank you for sharing paradise with me today."

He felt warmth creep up his arm, and his heartbeat kicked up a notch. Gracie's face was open and trusting. All he needed to do was tug on her hand and pull her forward and then cover her sweet mouth with his own. He squeezed her fingers gently and leaned forward a centimeter. "Thank you."

Gracie's eyes softened, and it seemed like she moved a fraction of an inch closer. If he kissed her now, how would that change things? Pika swallowed and noticed that the hollow of Gracie's throat twitched. Was she nervous to kiss him, or impatient? He smiled and moved closer, and then his phone vibrated with his daily alarm.

Pika glanced at his watch and groaned. The spell was broken. "Man, it's almost time for me to get chopping. Can we do something like this again sometime?"

Gracie smiled, but he thought he sensed disappointment in her eyes. Should he kiss her even though their moment had been interrupted? "I think we definitely should." She stepped back, and all hopes of kissing moved with her delicate feet. "I can't wait to see what else the island has to show me."

"I can't wait to be the one to show it to you," Pika responded before he thought better of it.

Gracie paused, turned her head, and nodded. "Deal." The sky opened up and rain began falling in a warm shower. She held out her hands and smiled up at the sky. "Even the rain is warm."

Pika chuckled. "We'd better get moving, or you'll be soaked."

"I don't mind."

All the way back to his pickup, Pika kept looking at Gracie and thinking of how he hoped that the house might need some extra work, because he would be done with the deck in a few short days. There definitely wasn't enough time to soak up Gracie's vibrant personality.

CHAPTER EIGHT

GRACIE

Gracie's energy continued to build for the rest of the day as she relived the moments where Pika had taken her hand, looked in her eyes, and almost kissed her. She was ninety-three percent certain that he had been thinking about kissing her, leaning in to kiss her, and *would* have kissed her if the alarm hadn't gone off on his phone. Even after the alarm, she was seventy-eight percent certain that he was still thinking about kissing her. She sighed. If only she had been brave enough to stand on her tiptoes and kiss him senseless. Gracie giggled—maybe all the fresh pineapple was getting to her.

Thinking of kissing Pika reminded Gracie of the fun pictures that Derek had taken of two sea turtles who appeared to be kissing. And that gave her the best idea for décor she'd had yet. The condo needed some personality, and she knew how to give it a personal touch that Lexi would love. She would take Derek's original photos plus the frames that Pika's mother, Kima, had woven, and she would hang them around the open kitchen and living room area. In the bedrooms, she could use some of Lexi's seascape paintings.

Her best friend claimed that the art she created was purely therapeutic, but Gracie had been admiring Lexi's work and wondering if the retired billionaire realized how talented she was. Gracie pulled out a box of paintings Lexi had tucked into a closet and breathed in the scent of oil paint and canvas. This was going to be perfect.

A few hours later, Gracie stood back to admire the work she'd accomplished. She had hung no less than twelve of Derek's photographs in various sizes around the living room. On one wall, she'd made a sort of collage with different-sized frames featuring all underwater shots. She loved the effect it gave the room. There were photos of sea turtles, brightly colored fish, coral, and even a whale.

In the guest bedroom, Gracie had highlighted Lexi's paintings and the room was much more inviting with seascapes, flowers, and luscious green trees painted with dainty orchids growing from their trunks. The simple canvas was painted with colors from the island palette. It drew Gracie in, and she felt a wave of nostalgia come over her. She remembered a time when her mother talked about the mighty ocean and how the waves danced across the seashore just like Gracie.

With a sigh, Gracie sank into the comfortable chair in the corner of the room. It had been fifteen years, but she still missed her mother. "I wish I could ask your advice right now, Mom," Gracie whispered. "I don't know if I'm doing the right thing—if this is where I'm supposed to be."

Gracie closed her eyes and pictured her mother's loving face. She had been much too young to go, and her death especially surprised everyone because her diabetes had seemed to be under control. She had attended Gracie's first performance of Odette in Tchaikovsky's *Swan Lake* and been moved to tears as she praised her daughter's talents.

"You are a star!" her mother had gushed. "You were the most beautiful dancer up there. You have the ability to do whatever your heart desires. Don't forget that, Gracie."

She'd died in her sleep that night, and Gracie had never forgotten her mother's words.

With a start, Gracie sat up in the chair. All this time, she'd thought of her "ability" as strictly related to dance, but as she replayed those final words in her memory, it was as if her mother was whispering to her to listen closer. She had the ability to do *whatever her heart desired*—what if that wasn't dance anymore?

Gracie stood and walked around the room, admiring Lexi's paintings. Her friend had radically changed her life and was doing something completely different now. Lexi used to work at a grueling pace in her brother's importing and exporting business through China, but now she'd created an arm of Burke Enterprises called Burke's Higher Steps that reached an entirely different part of the world.

Could Gracie find and cultivate a new ability here on this beautiful island? Not only that, but there was an even more important question she kept asking herself: could she be happy if she wasn't dancing on the stage?

GRACIE

The next morning, Gracie's heart leapt like a dolphin in the salty waves when Pika pulled up a little after seven to start working on the deck. She was excited, yet tentative to show him the work that she'd done in decorating the house. Right after Pika knocked on the door, Gracie's throat constricted in a panic. What if he didn't like what she had done? Pika and Derek were best friends, so that meant that Pika would have a pretty good read on whether Gracie had made the right move or not. She swallowed and pushed the doubts from her mind as she walked toward the front door.

"Mahalo," Pika said as he walked through the door. "It's a beautiful morning—whoa, you've been busy here." He dropped his tool bag and stepped toward the wall, examining the photos.

Gracie held her breath as he walked past each one.

He turned to her and smiled. "This looks good."

"Do you really think so? Or are you just saying that?"

"It's like a showcase for Derek and a theme for the house. You did good."

Gracie bit her bottom lip and danced in place. "I was so worried, but excited at the same time. Want to see what I did with the bedroom?"

"There's more? You've been busy. Good thing you don't chop coconuts, or I'd be out of a job."

She laughed and felt all the stress melt off her shoulders. "I decided to be a little risky and feature Lexi's art in here."

Pika walked through the doorway of the bedroom and nodded. "They are going to love this. I heard Derek tell Lexi that she has talent, but she won't believe him."

"Right? Why does she doubt herself? I love her style."

Pika looked at her and his mouth twitched.

"What?"

He lifted one shoulder and let it drop. "Interesting that what you say about your friend could be true for other people too."

Gracie furrowed her brow. "You mean me?"

Pika winked. "I'd better get to work. You're putting me to shame."

"Whatever. That deck probably is better than it was brand-new." Gracie tsked. "I wonder who else certain things could be true for..."

Pika halted, and she could see the moment he understood what she meant. His eyes softened, and at the same time he bolted into action, nearly colliding with the glass door to the patio.

He got right to work, and Gracie surreptitiously

watched him, thinking about their conversation. His praise was genuine, and she felt a mountain of pressure slide off into the ocean. She really could do this. She could decorate a Hawaiian bungalow with beauty, appeal, and a unique flair that guests would love. Her heart bloomed with happiness that she hadn't felt in months.

Now, if only Pika could see the same thing about himself. She had sensed more than once that he felt somewhat ashamed about the hard labor he did. If he didn't realize how talented he was, then perhaps he was second-guessing himself too.

A few hours later, Pika came in to cool off. Gracie mixed up some lemonade, and Pika guzzled half the pitcher of sweet drink.

"You've been working hard. I don't know how you stand the humidity when it gets hot," Gracie said.

He shrugged. "I'm used to it, but yeah, this lemonade tastes good today. But maybe that has something to do with you."

Gracie ducked her head and smiled. She heard Pika's low chuckle. He seemed to enjoy making her blush.

"Hey, I wondered if you'd like to come fishing with me tomorrow afternoon, and then we could go back to my place and cook?"

Gracie's smile brightened. "I would love that. I still remember deep-sea fishing with you. I was scared to death the lines would break."

"Yeah, this will be a little different. You'll see." He tilted his head. "Do you know how to snorkel?"

"I've gone a few times. I wouldn't call myself an expert."

"You'll be fine, then. Wear your swimsuit, and I'll bring the gear."

Her heart spun, swirled, and expanded with excitement before she remembered that Pika had another job. "What about chopping coconuts at Ke'e?"

"Tomorrow, Jefe's cousin is coming into town and wanted to work. He'll be happy to take my place for a few hours." Pika thumbed behind him toward the deck. "I've been putting in a lot of extra hours with this project. My makuahine say I'm trying to kill myself working."

Gracie paused, remembering that makuahine meant mother. "Well, I'm glad your mother inspired you to take a break, then."

"Tomorrow, then. I'll stop by here between three and four o'clock."

"Sounds good," Gracie replied, trying to remain calm as her toes itched to dance the melody singing through her veins.

Pika gave her hand a squeeze on his way out the door. Gracie waited until he drove away to give in to the urge to dance. Her limbs stretched into familiar rhythms, but her heart was beating out an entirely new rhythm, and it was exquisitely pleasant.

CHAPTER TEN

PIKA

On his way home after a long day of work, Pika thought about what he needed to do to prepare for Gracie to see his house tomorrow. His gut tightened when he considered the contrasts of his life and Gracie's. He was happy to have a home to live in, but he was worried about what Gracie might think of it. Pika had worked every morning on Derek's house for six months to repair the run-down hut. Derek's kupuna, or grandpa, had left the house to Derek, and it had been a lifeline while the two friends worked to make ends meet on the island. About the time Derek met Lexi, the house had been falling apart and in need of a new roof. Derek hadn't been certain that they could continue living there for another year. Then he'd married a billionaire and those problems disappeared like the clouds on a sunny day.

Restoring the old home had been a labor of love, and Derek had insisted that Pika live there and pay rent that was well below what they could have collected. He assured him that it wasn't charity because Pika had worked harder than anyone else they could find on the island. It was true that construction work wasn't the first choice of most of his native friends, but the world continued to change and Kauai changed with it. The island was growing, and there always seemed to be more demand than workers to fill the need.

He was grateful to have a roof over his head that didn't leak, although he missed his old roommate. Derek was a solid friend with a lot of talent and grit. His photography business was a success, and that didn't have anything to do with Lexi's money. Pika wanted to be like his friends—successful, yet down to earth. He wanted to have enough for his needs, yet still have time to enjoy the beauty of the island that had always been his home. He'd made a lot of mistakes in his life when it came to work, finances, and being a bit reckless.

He tightened his grip on the steering wheel. What if pursuing Gracie was another one of his stupid mistakes?

TRAFFIC COMING down from the north shore was busier than Pika would have liked, but nothing he shouldn't have expected on a Friday afternoon. He had been working for the past five hours chopping coconuts, and he couldn't wait to see Gracie again. He was still a little nervous about taking Gracie to his house, but he was excited about the fishing they would do beforehand. He was fairly certain that Gracie had never seen anything like spearfishing before. He would stop by his place to change into swim trunks and grab his fishing gear, which included snorkeling gear and an extra net for Gracie to help him bring in the fish.

Pika pulled into the driveway, and before he could make it to the front door, Gracie was coming down the steps to meet him with a bright smile. "Aloha," she said. Her dark hair was pulled back into a ponytail, and she wore black shorts over her dark pink swimsuit.

"Aloha." Pika smiled, and for a minute all of his nerves faded away. "I guess this means you're ready?"

"I've been looking forward to this all day," Gracie answered with her signature laugh. The musical quality to it made Pika think he was in exactly the right place.

"Me too." He put his arm around her shoulders and gave her a little squeeze. "You are beautiful."

"Thank you," Gracie murmured, leaning her head into his shoulder. "So are you."

Pika chuckled. This woman was unlike any other he'd ever dated. She was absolutely gorgeous and didn't have trouble speaking her mind. He'd also never been called beautiful before, but it had him standing up a bit straighter next to the willowy beauty.

Once they were in his pickup and back on the road, Gracie turned to him. "Are you going to tell me where we're going?"

"We're headed to Beach House beach for some fishing. Have you heard of it?"

Gracie nodded. "Yeah, I've seen tons of sunset pictures

posted by friends who have dined at that restaurant. It seems pretty fancy. I didn't know there was fishing nearby."

"That's the fun part. I'm going to show you another way I like to fish. Spearfishing."

"Oh, like with the harpoon?"

Pika shrugged. "Yeah, except I use a speargun. It's pretty cool." He chatted with her about the basics of spearfishing as they drove. "I dive with fins and mask, and I wear a weighted belt. I wait for the right fish and pull the trigger."

When they reached Beach House, he parked on the side of the road and pulled the gear out of the back of his pickup. He handed Gracie the snorkeling gear, then took out his spear gun and showed it to her. "This is sort of like an underwater bow and arrow. See, I put the spear in place and then release it here and hope that I can hit a fish."

"How many tries does it usually take?"

"Depends on how friendly the fish are feeling. There are usually a bigger variety just around the reef. They like to hide in the rocks. Derek and I used to fish here a lot. The weather is beautiful, so either way, I think you'll enjoy the snorkeling."

"I think there's something very humbling about wearing snorkeling gear," Gracie said as she lifted up the mask.

Pika chuckled. "Good thing you don't have anything to worry about." He shouldered the rest of his gear, and they walked down to the beach. The tide was on its way in, and the sun was working on its descent across the horizon. "We're going to do a little swimming." He led the way to the dock that ran alongside the restaurant. "This will be a shorter fishing trip than some, because we want to eat dinner, not just catch it."

Gracie peered out at the water. "I'm excited. Let's go!"

He helped Gracie check her mask for a good seal and gave her a few tips before they started swimming. "Just hang back a little and you'll see. But I do want you to help me net the fish." He handed her the net, and she gripped it tightly, nodding. He snapped on his weight belt and stepped off the dock with a splash.

They swam about fifteen feet from the dock, and Pika reached out to squeeze Gracie's fingertips. She turned towards him and gave him a thumbs-up. Then she pointed behind him excitedly. He turned and saw a school of brightly colored fish swimming towards him and a gray shape behind them that indicated he might be able to make a good fish dinner. He lifted his head up and gulped a breath of air before diving down, readying his aim. He released the trigger, but it went wide, missing his target. He pulled the spear back in and let his head pop above water as he reloaded.

Gracie floated in the water next to him. She lifted up her mask. "This is so cool. I saw the fish you were aiming for. Honestly, if you hit one, I think you're going to be the most talented man I know. I can't imagine ever being able to catch a fish this way."

Pika laughed. "Well, if that's all it takes, I should have taken you fishing on our first date. But really, you should see some of my friends. They have a sense about it, and they can hit a fish the first time."

"That's awesome. I'm watching so I can learn," Gracie said.

"Do you want to try it?" Pika held out the speargun.

She shook her head. "Not today. But definitely next time."

Pika nodded and dove back underwater. He tried twice more, aiming for an ono and a smaller mahi mahi that would be pretty impressive to Gracie. He came up for air, and Gracie followed him.

"What about that funny blue fish that looked like it had buckteeth?" She pointed beneath the surface. "There seem to be a lot of those."

"Those are parrotfish. We'll steer clear in this area, as they might have ciguatera."

"What's that?"

"It's basically poison." Pika swam closer to her. "The fish that are higher up on the food chain become toxic from a microalgae. Jefe still eats them, but he is careful about what parts he cooks. I'd rather just go for the mahi mahi or the tuna."

"Poison? Like you'll die from it?"

"Nah, but cig makes you pretty miserable and can affect you neurologically. See, these are the things people depend on the natives to know." He adjusted his spear.

"I'm glad I have you." Gracie lifted the net. "I'm ready to go again. Are you?"

Pika felt his heart rate speed up. This woman didn't need a net to catch him. He was already a goner. "Let's go."

Gracie nodded and adjusted her mask. She basically floated on top of the water with her head just below the surface watching him. He swam around looking for a good target and tried three more times before he finally hit a good-sized ono.

When he surfaced, Gracie had her mask off and was

cheering. "You did it! That was so cool." She held the net out, and he put the fish in. It was probably about sixteen inches long.

He loved her enthusiasm, and he especially loved what a natural she was at doing something that Hawaiian natives didn't think twice about. "I'd like to get a couple more fish to cook up for my family. Let's see how lucky I am today."

"What kind are you hoping to spear?"

"Definitely kumu," Pika replied. "The pink fish are called kumu, or goatfish, and they are my tutu's favorite."

Twenty minutes later, he had four fish and one very excited Gracie ready to head out for a fish fry. "I think the timing will be right for cooking fish during a beautiful sunset," he said.

Gracie smiled. "I can't wait."

They left the beach just as the dinner rush was beginning. Pika was happy to be headed in the opposite direction. When he pulled up to his modest home, he watched Gracie from the corner of his eye.

"This is a nice area. You're so close to the beach. I bet you love that for surfing."

"It is the best of both worlds, although some days I really hate the drive up to the north shore. Luckily, there's plenty of good surfing up there to pay me back for my drive." He hopped out of his pickup to get Gracie's door, and then they carried the fish around back.

He gutted and cleaned the fish, and Gracie surprised him by her interest in the process. "I thought you'd be freaked out by this," he admitted.

"No, my dad is a big fisherman. I bet he would go nuts over the size of these fish."

Pika grinned. This woman was full of surprises. He watched her as she helped prepare vegetables to go with their meal. Each movement spoke of her delicate, yet strong manner. She caught him watching her and smiled, a hint of blush tinting her cheeks. How would it feel to hold her close and kiss her? Pika bit his lower lip—best to get the fish fried before his thoughts took him any further.

CHAPTER ELEVEN

GRACIE

Gracie couldn't stop thinking about the way Pika had looked at her while they'd been preparing the fish. Wonder and adoration were the words she would use to describe the soft way he assessed her, and it felt oh so good. He didn't care whether she was a star ballet dancer or a slightly clumsy net-holder for a fisherman. She felt freer than she had in years. And definitely fuller too—the delicious fish Pika had fried reminded her of the fish fry where she'd met Pika last year.

They ate outside under an interesting bottle palm tree sitting in the patchy grass that grew haphazardly in the yard. The tree appeared to be in the shape of a bottle with palm fronds coming out of the top.

"What was your favorite fish?" Pika asked.

"Definitely the goatfish kumu one. It was so tender and flaky." Gracie stretched out her legs and wiggled her toes.

"So you fish, surf, chop coconuts, and work construction. What else does Pika Sepe want to do when he grows up?"

Pika finished chewing and leaned against the tree. "Well, all the Hawaiian things, of course."

"Which are?"

"More surfing, swimming, fishing, sleeping in the sun—that sort of thing."

Gracie elbowed him. "And?"

He paused, seeming to consider his words. With a glance in her direction, he blew out a breath. "I've thought about starting my own business—ya know, for the tourists."

"Really?" Gracie sat up. Pika looked nervous about revealing his secret, but she wanted him to know that she was truly interested in him and his ideas. "What kind of business? Like a private tour?"

"Sort of. Giving them the island experience from my point of view. Not just the big highlights, but the little things, our way of life."

"Pika, that's exactly what I want to learn about the island. Remember when I said that very thing?" She sidled up next to him. "Hmm, where would you take me first?"

Pika chuckled. "Some of the places we've already been. Fishing and my makuahine's famous fish fry. Art night in Hanapepe. The bamboo forest. Paddle-boarding where the river meets the ocean. Hiking along Na Pali, snorkeling tunnels. Maybe some surfing."

"That sounds like quite the adventure. Where do I sign up?"

"Do you really think someone would want to go with a smaller tour?" He lifted his arm and put it around her shoulder.

She loved the way his large hands covered her, how safe and secure she felt in that moment. "And have a native with a personal touch guiding them? Why not?"

Pika shrugged. "I even thought about getting Derek involved with some underwater photography shoots. We talked about it back in the day."

"I think you should try. What would it hurt to put your idea out there and test it?"

"Aw, I'm not sure I know where to even start."

Gracie tilted her head to look in his eyes. "Meaning what? You don't know where to start? Or you're afraid to start?"

Pika flinched. "You cut to the core, wahine." He gave her a playful squeeze. "A bit of both, and of course there's a website, social media, flyers, stuff like that."

"I understand that would seem daunting, but remember that you're connected to a few experts in that area."

He glanced up into the trees, thinking it over, and then looked back at her. "You're right. Maybe I should see if Derek still likes the idea. Thanks for listening to me."

Gracie patted his arm and left her hand on top of his forearm, the corded muscles firm under her fingertips. "Fo' sho."

Pika chuckled and leaned toward her. "You're something else, ya know?"

"Yeah?" she said, her voice husky. There was something in his eyes, a desire that he didn't try to hide. He glanced at her mouth, and Gracie moved a fraction of an inch closer, so that his breath was hot on her lips.

"Yeah," Pika said as he covered her mouth with his full lips.

The kiss electrified her soul, and Gracie pressed her lips against his while tracing her fingers along the back of his neck. She tasted salt and sweetness and felt his strength as he wrapped his brawny arms around her and pulled her closer. Pika kissed either side of her mouth and then her lips again as he pulled her onto his lap. The trees swayed gently in the breeze above them, and the ocean crashed in the background. It felt like his heart was pressed up against hers, beating in tandem. Every kiss sang to her soul, and Gracie forgot her worries and fears and left them lying in the grass under Pika's trees.

CHAPTER TWELVE

PIKA

Pika had kissed plenty of girls, but nothing could compare to kissing Gracie. It took all of his strength to stop kissing her and take her back home. He walked her up to the front door, thinking that there was no way he was leaving without another kiss. Gracie touched her lips with her fingertips, obviously thinking the same thing.

"Gracie, tonight was the best. Can I see you again tomorrow?"

"You'd better. That deck isn't going to be completed without you." She lifted her eyebrows and smirked.

Pika covered her smirk with a kiss. He'd almost forgotten that tomorrow he would be back to finish up the deck. How would he be able to keep his hands off this gorgeous woman?

As if reading his thoughts, Gracie leaned back and

murmured, "I'll kiss you before I have to run some errands tomorrow, but then I want you to take me somewhere when you get off work."

"Yeah? Where?" He would literally go anywhere she asked. He breathed her in, a scent with something sweet and spicy—just how he would describe Gracie.

"A hike? The beach? It doesn't matter where. I just want to be with you."

Pika was thinking the beach would be nice: lying on the hot sand and kissing Gracie—well, probably not the beach. "Maybe we hike to the first overlook over Ke'e Beach and see what we think?"

"Should I bring dinner?"

"Anything you'd like." Pika kissed her, pulling her closer into an embrace. She sighed as he deepened the kiss, and for a moment, he wondered how he could leave her alone for the night. Then he remembered his grandma. She would love Gracie, and she would also beat him senseless if he was anything less than a gentleman with this precious woman. Pika kissed Gracie once more and took in a breath. "I'm going to go home now, but I will see you tomorrow as much as you'll let me."

Gracie giggled. "Oh, you're going to see me a lot, then. Good night, Pika."

Man, he was whipped. He waved at her as she closed the front door. Why he'd ever let her out of his life last year was a mystery he didn't care to solve. She was here now, and he would make sure she knew he wanted her to stay.

～

THE NEXT MORNING, just after six o'clock, Pika's phone chirped with a text. He smiled, wondering if it could be Gracie. He flipped over the phone and groaned when he saw that it was from Leilani.

Hey, my man. I love you so much! I can't wait to see you. Are you busy tonight?

Pika shook his head. He needed to tell Gracie about his ex-girlfriend, because the crazy woman didn't know what breaking up meant. With a grunt, he sent a short, but powerful reply:

I don't want to see you anymore. We are NOT dating. You are NOT my girlfriend. Stop this or I will block your number.

Almost immediately, Leilani responded.

I just want to talk. I don't understand why we can't be friends?

Pika's fingers hovered over his phone. She wasn't going to take no for an answer. Time to show her that he wasn't playing games.

Blocking you now. Goodbye.

He glared at his phone as he quickly tapped to the screen to block Leilani's number. His heart twisted in his chest, because he didn't want to hurt her. At the same time, he felt a sense of relief once he'd blocked Leilani. Things had gotten way off track, and he still wasn't quite sure how it had happened. He liked Gracie too much to risk their budding relationship with texts from an old girlfriend.

CHAPTER THIRTEEN

GRACIE

Gracie's heart fluttered whenever she thought of Pika. He'd arrived at the house just after seven, and after one quick peck he'd promised to stay out of her way and get his work done so they could play later. Her face heated up when she thought of how much she wanted to be kissing him instead of working.

She followed his lead and knuckled down with her design ideas to finish up the bungalow. She hung new curtains, arranged throw pillows, and readjusted some knickknacks she was using as focal pieces in each room. The house was almost ready, and Gracie loved the ambience she'd created there. Peaceful, relaxing, and yet invigorating were words she would choose to describe the living space. Gracie made a few more notes of what she needed to complete the look she had created for the home. She had driven by a few flea markets in the past week, and she wanted to see if she might be able to find an interesting piece today for the coffee table in the living room.

"I'm done here for today." Pika came in from the patio and jolted her from her thoughts of interior design. "Are you still okay with meeting me at Ke'e Beach about five?"

Gracie tilted her head to one side. "I'm a little sad that I have to wait until five, but I'll be a good girl and get my chores done. I'm planning to stop by a few flea markets to find some unique pieces to decorate the living room. Too bad you can't help me with that."

Pika grinned and came toward her. In three steps, he reached her and wrapped his muscular arms around her, pulling her close. "Don't tempt me. I'm trying to be a good boy, too."

She giggled and leaned forward, pressing a chaste kiss to his mouth. "Okay, I won't," she murmured.

Pika groaned and leaned his head down, resting his forehead against hers. "You get that I really like you, ya?"

A thousand butterflies took flight in her chest at his words. He really liked her—there was no doubt now. She'd come back to Kauai suffering from the loss of her career, and now this gorgeous Hawaiian was carefully filling that hole. Her heart thrummed with joy. She put her hand on his cheek. "I think so. You get that I like you too?"

"Mm, hmm." Pika's voice rumbled in his chest. He kissed her lips and then her cheek. "I'll see you later."

"Good luck today." Gracie held the door open for him as he exited with his tools.

"You too. I hope you find what you're looking for."

"Oh, trust me, I'll find it."

Pika chuckled as he walked down the steps. Gracie

forced herself to close the door and walk back to the living room. She picked up her notebook with sketches and notes on decorating and held it to her chest. She lifted up on her toes and twirled around. Pika liked her! It might just be her favorite day yet in Hawaii.

GRACIE MADE plans to hit the flea markets on her way up to the north shore. There were several, and Saturday was described as a busy day with more fare from various vendors. She wasn't sure what she was looking for, but when she saw it, she would know.

Sprouting Horn Park boasted a great array of merchandise both new and old, and since it was right next to Poipu in Koloa, Gracie stopped there first. The ocean waves made a beautiful backdrop to the setting of the market. The air was mild with a floral scent that Gracie hoped she'd never get used to. There were about a dozen people milling about the booths, chatting with vendors. Some of the stuff was the regular cheap souvenirs that often were made in China and sold as if they were authentic Hawaiian fare. Interspersed between the obligatory souvenirs, Gracie sought out vendors with handmade creations indicative of the island.

Beautiful black pearl bracelets, shell necklaces, and earrings with some type of natural wood caught her eye. She bent over a glass case with black pearl bracelets interspersed with other stones. She noted the price tag of seventy-five dollars and pulled her bottom lip through her teeth. The price was a little high for her uncertain budget at the moment, but that didn't stop her from wondering how it might be to own a piece like it.

"You're welcome to try that on. It would look lovely with your skin tone."

Gracie looked up and met the dark eyes of the vendor. His eyes were framed with long, dark lashes, and he stood well over six feet tall. His Polynesian frame filled up the area, reminding her of Pika. "Thank you. Do these pearls hold up to everyday wear?"

He nodded and carefully removed a bracelet. "Not so much that. Pearls are alive. You don't want them to come into contact with cosmetics, perfume, that sort of thing. If you store them correctly, take care of them ... they last forever."

Gracie slid the bracelet on her arm. "They really are beautiful."

"Would go well with a beautiful woman wearing them," the man said.

Gracie kept her head down, examining the bracelet. "Thank you." She stared at the pearls wistfully. It would be fun to have a piece like this someday, but that wasn't what she was looking for. She removed it and returned it to the case. "Thank you for letting me try it on."

"Of course," his deep voice rumbled. "Maybe you will come back and look again?"

Gracie lifted her right shoulder and let it fall. "Maybe."

"Ah, maybe. Well, maybe I shouldn't say, but you seem like a nice woman."

"Huh?" Gracie hesitated, trying to understand what he was talking about.

"You have to be careful around here." He lowered his

voice. "Some men like to take advantage of the tourists for a little island romance."

Gracie stepped back. The guy was handsome, but cryptic, and she wasn't in the mood for games. She straightened her shoulders. "What do you mean?"

"Weren't you fishing with Pika Sepe last night at Beach House?"

Gracie's eyes widened at the mention of Pika. "Who are you?"

"I'm Brave Kamai." The man flashed her another dazzling smile and extended his hand. "And you?"

"How do you know Pika?" It wasn't entirely surprising that this man would know him, because Pika had grown up on the south side of the island. Kauai wasn't as densely populated as some of the other islands of Hawaii.

"We go way back—grew up in the same neighborhood," Brave replied. "He's never wanted to settle down, but he's great at fishing, if you know what I mean." Brave tapped his heart and pointed at her. "Catch and release."

Gracie narrowed her eyes. She didn't like this man and what he was insinuating. "Actually, I don't know what you mean. Pika is a good friend to a couple of my best friends. I met him last year, and he definitely doesn't strike me as the type of fisherman you're describing."

Brave shrugged. "Give him time. You'll see."

Gracie turned to go, but then paused and said, "I'm not a tourist, by the way. I live here. You might think twice about your business before you speak." She spun on her heel and walked across the market.

The other vendors held no interest for her, as she walked with hands trembling to her car. Who was Brave

Kamai, and why would he speak ill of Pika? Gracie had never seen even a hint of malice in the man who made her heart swell with his gentle embraces and sweet kisses. She would remember Brave and ask Pika about him as soon as she arrived at Ke'e Beach.

CHAPTER FOURTEEN

PIKA

It had proved to be one of the busiest Saturdays Pika had seen in a month. The weather was perfect for hiking, and he and Jefe could hardly keep up with the demand for fresh-chopped coconut waters. Usually, they were able to chop a few coconuts ahead of time and keep them in coolers in the pickup, but there had been a line of three to six people for the past two hours. The demand from the heat had brought on extra tips, and as the afternoon wore on, Pika began to wonder if business would slow down enough for him to take off at five.

He chopped the husk of the coconut off as fast as he could, but every time he looked up, the line seemed to get longer. "Man, we need Derek here today."

Jefe looked up and laughed. "Nah, he'd cut into our profits. Business is good, bro. We're keeping up okay."

Pika grunted and kept chopping. Jefe used to be his

main competitor for the hot spot at the base of the hiking trail, but that all changed when Derek had met Lexi and his photography business had taken off. Pika thought about how he had shared his business ideas with Gracie. She hadn't laughed or scorned his idea as too small or dreamy, the way Leilani had. Gracie had encouraged him to try. But as sweat ran down his back with every stroke of his knife, he wondered how he would have the time or energy to build a separate business.

Jefe was older and he wouldn't be able to keep up on his own, but he did have a couple of sons who helped out sometimes. Maybe they could work a few more hours to offset Pika's absence *if* he decided to try something new. "Hey," Pika said, "maybe you should call one of your boys and have them come and help. I have a date at five, and it doesn't look like we're going to be slowing down anytime soon."

Jefe peered at him with a half-smile. "A date?"

"Shut up." Pika waved his machete in Jefe's direction, and the old man chuckled.

"I'll make a call."

Pika grinned and shook his head. Jefe might razz him a little, but Gracie was worth it. He fell back into his rhythmic chopping, and Jefe shared his grizzled smile with customers.

"I've never known Pika to leave work for a date. This must be some woman," Jefe ventured.

"She is. Now get back to work."

Thankfully, they were too busy for much small talk, so Pika was able to avoid further questions about his date. He found himself watching the road as the sun edged lower in the sky. With no rain on the horizon, more people arrived at the beach to hike, swim, and snorkel.

Ten coconuts later, he saw Gracie walking toward his pickup. She wore khaki shorts and a red tank top that set off her dark hair. Pika paused and lifted his hand in a wave. Gracie smiled brightly and picked up her step as she approached him.

"You must be the lady who has Pika chopping coconuts backwards today," Jefe said.

Gracie laughed. "I thought he was so good, he could chop forwards and backwards and no one would know the difference?"

Pika fell a little harder for her right then. "Gracie, have you met Jefe before?"

"I don't think so." She reached out a hand. "I'm Gracie Cardulo. I'm new on the island."

"Ah, and the first guy you met was Pika, huh? Too bad you couldn't have found my sons first. They're much better-looking."

Pika snorted, and Gracie covered her mouth as she laughed. "You know there is more to Pika than good looks, though, right? He holds a machete, but he's gentle and kind, too."

Jefe's face softened, and he looked toward Pika. "Better hold on to that one."

"Thanks, Jefe. Will Akoni be here soon?"

"Any minute. Go on."

"Give me a sec," he said to Gracie. She nodded, and Pika quickly chopped two more coconuts and readied them for sale. He hopped out of the back of the pickup and brushed his hands on his shorts. "Ready?"

"Fo' sho," Gracie replied.

Pika tickled her side, and she shrieked and ran ahead a few steps. "You're that ticklish?"

"Nope. Definitely not." Gracie held out her hand and grasped his fingers. "It looks like you had a really busy day."

"And you must be really ticklish to work so hard to change the subject and keep my hands occupied." He reached around with his left hand and grabbed her side.

"Pika! No fair." She jumped and yanked on his hand, making him stumble on the uneven path.

"Okay, okay." He lifted up his hand and tugged her toward him. "How about this instead?" He leaned down and kissed her.

Gracie put her hand on his chest and let out a little sigh as she kissed him back. "I like that much better," she breathed.

"We were just planning to go sit on the beach and make out, right?"

Gracie shoved him to the side. "C'mon. Tell me about this side of the island."

Pika put his hand on the small of her back and guided her toward the trailhead. "The north shore typically has rougher ocean in the winter—but still not too bad. There are some great surf and snorkel spots. And the mountains here are beautiful." They began climbing as Pika talked. "This trail is steep at first and then switches back and forth. We're just going to the first overlook because I've chopped too many coconuts today."

"Everything is so green. It rained here today, didn't it?" Gracie pointed out a puddle at the base of a tree.

"Yeah, this morning, but not at your house. Pretty typical. Some people say it's always raining somewhere on the island. I'm actually surprised at how well the weather has held all afternoon."

They chatted as they continued the steep climb up the mountain. Gracie stepped carefully to avoid the red mud and tree roots crisscrossing the path. Pika loved watching how gracefully she moved even as she hiked up the mountainside. He was about to ask her about life as a ballerina, but hesitated. Even though he truly wanted to know more about her and her life, he didn't want to dredge up sadness.

"I had something odd happen today when I stopped at the flea market by Poipu."

Pika gave himself a mental shake as Gracie pulled him from his thoughts. "What was that?"

"I was looking at some jewelry, a black pearl bracelet, and the man warned me about you."

"What?" Pika stared at Gracie, making sure he'd heard her right. "Who was he?"

"Brave Kamai. Do you know him?"

Pika groaned and held in the expletive he wanted to say. "Yes, I know him well. I dated his younger sister and broke up with her recently."

Gracie bit her bottom lip. "Okay, so he hates you now?"

"Yeah, I guess. We grew up together and I dated Leilani for a few months, but she got all lolo—I mean crazy, and started acting like we were already engaged—wanted to plan the wedding."

Gracie's eyes widened. "Oh goodness."

"She's a drama queen. I liked her, but not like that. It got weird, and she keeps calling and texting me. I actually blocked her number. I'm guessing that probably gave her some things to say about me."

Gracie was quiet for a moment as they walked.

"I'm sorry. I planned to tell you about her because I wanted you to know that I'm not messing around. Now it feels all awkward." Pika wanted to punch Brave about now. "Wait, how did Brave even know who you were?"

"That's what I wondered. He asked for my name, and I didn't tell him. He said he saw us fishing at Beach House last night." Gracie stopped and turned toward Pika. "Do you still have feelings for her? Because I don't want to get in the way of that."

"What? No!" Pika put his forehead in his hand and blew out a breath. "This is coming out all wrong. I tried to break up with Leilani before, but she wouldn't take no for an answer. I am not interested in her romantically. I love her family. It's sad that Brave is acting that way, but he *is* her older brother." Pika lifted his head and looked Gracie in the eyes. "I'm sorry."

She blinked a few times, as if clearing her eyes. Man, if he made her cry, he was going to slam Brave next time they crossed paths. Gracie put her hand on his arm. "It's okay. It's awkward, but I think I understand. Brave told me that you liked to go after tourists for an island fling."

Pika punched his palm. "That guy is gonna miss his face next time we meet."

Gracie smiled. "Nah, I already told him off. Let's not worry about him or your ex-girlfriend. We're on a date."

"You told him off?"

Gracie started walking again and looked over her shoulder with a wink. "I know you, Pika. Some random dude with an ax to grind isn't going to change how I feel about you."

Pika's mouth dropped open. No words, just his heart rocking in his chest, telling him to take note of this woman. He took two steps and grabbed her hand. "Thanks, Gracie. That means a lot." He squeezed her fingers gently.

She nodded, and they walked the last few steps to the rise that overlooked Ke'e Beach. Gracie gasped as they turned and took in the vista of beautiful ocean meeting the gray-blue sky. The beach slithered along the coast with the mountains rising up around it. "It's so beautiful."

The ocean sparkled under the bright sun, and Pika looked around for signs of clouds. "That's Na Pali Coast, and over there in that dark green jungle is where it rains every day—Waialeale." He pointed across the beach toward the mountains. Above the Waialeale crater, the usual rain clouds hovered, but unless a wind brought them over, the two of them could probably finish their hike without getting wet. Pika put his arm around Gracie, tilting his head toward her. "Yes, it is, but it doesn't compare to you."

Gracie turned and leaned up on her tiptoes to kiss him. Pika kissed her and hoped that they could hold on to this moment. Something told him that the trouble stirring with Leilani wasn't over, but he had weathered other storms. He held Gracie tighter. Everything felt different with her, and he wasn't going to let her go.

CHAPTER FIFTEEN

GRACIE

Sunday was a perfect day on the island of Kauai, but it wasn't the weather that made it so perfect. It was Pika. If Gracie was being honest with herself, she was falling hard for the handsome Hawaiian. He picked her up at nine, and they attended church services in Kalaheo. Gracie noticed a few looks when she walked in next to Pika and they sat in a pew. The bench groaned under the weight of his muscular body. Gracie had a hard time concentrating on the sermon, because she was thinking of how it felt to be held in his arms.

Pika lifted his arm and put it around her shoulders, and she leaned into his side. Last night, they had hiked back down to the beach and walked along collecting driftwood as they'd talked. She felt like they could have stayed up all night talking—and, of course, kissing. Pika had been a gentleman and taken her home, not even coming inside. It was a beautiful feeling knowing that he respected her, and she wanted him to know that she felt the same way about him.

Her ballet career had made it difficult to date with the grueling practices and travel away from her hometown. She'd only had a couple of semi-serious relationships, and neither of those had made her feel the way she did now. With a glance at Pika, she turned and attempted to focus on the sermon.

The preacher spoke of God's love for His children, of how vast and infinite it was. "No matter what you do, God will never stop loving you. This is a love that is often hard for us to understand for ourselves and others. Satan wants us to believe that God cannot love a broken person, but nothing is further from the truth."

Pika squeezed Gracie's shoulder. He seemed to be listening intently to the sermon. Maybe that was part of Pika's secret to what appeared to be the relaxed, Hawaiian way of life. Perhaps he understood how much God loved him and that was enough. Gracie let the words swirl around her heart. How would life feel if she believed the same sentiment—that despite challenges, loss, and heartbreaking mistakes, God still loved her?

The preacher cleared his throat. "Let God's love be enough for you. Don't go searching for fulfillment from the world. True happiness comes from only one place. When you accept that, you'll feel freer than you ever have before."

That was the kind of description Gracie wanted for her life—to be free. To love, to dance if the opportunity presented itself, but to truly be free to live her life. She leaned against Pika again and put her small hand on his thigh. Maybe this was her chance to truly start living, here under the Hawaiian sun with Pika. Her heart fluttered and she mentally shook herself. No need to get carried away, but she would enjoy this gift while she could.

After the service, Pika steered her through the pews, greeting some of the other parishioners. He stopped in front of a middle-aged woman dressed in a bright purple muumuu. "Gracie, I'd like you to meet my mother, Kima."

Gracie's stomach lurched. Pika was introducing her to his mother without warning? She smiled brightly. "Aloha. I'm happy to meet you. Your son is one of the kindest people I know."

Kima studied her for a brief second, and then her face softened. She returned the smile. "Aloha. I've never heard him talk about anyone the way he does you, Gracie." She turned to Pika. "You've told her about Leilani?"

"Mom," Pika groaned. "Yes, I've told her about my ex-girlfriend, because that's what all people love to talk about when they are dating someone new."

Gracie laughed, but she watched Kima closely. It seemed the woman might not be entirely happy about the fact that Leilani was an ex-girlfriend.

"What are your plans for the rest of the day?" Kima asked. "Would you like to come over for dinner?"

Gracie opened her mouth to answer, but Pika beat her to it. "Thanks, Mom, but we have other plans. Rain check?"

Kima narrowed her eyes. "This time, but a mother likes to see her son once in a while."

Pika kissed his mother's cheek. "Soon. Love you."

"Love you too, dear." She hugged Pika and then smiled at Gracie. "Have a good day."

"Thank you. And you as well." Gracie followed Pika to the end of the pew before whispering, "Anyone else we're going to meet without warning?"

Pika grinned. "I'm avoiding the Kamai family today. I don't think they're ready to meet you. I hope you don't mind."

"That's probably a good idea." Gracie looked up then and locked eyes with Brave. His brows were furrowed and he frowned, but she smiled brightly in his direction and gripped Pika's arm.

They exited the building before they could run into Brave, and Gracie was glad. As they drove away, Pika took her hand. "I'm sorry that I introduced you to my mother without warning. I didn't want you to stress."

"Oh, how nice of you. FYI, in the future, if you don't want me to stress, warn me that I'm going to meet a *significant* member of your family." Gracie arched her eyebrow and allowed a little bite into her tone.

Pika lifted his hands up and chuckled. "Okay, okay. I'm sorry. Well, actually, I should confess that I didn't want to stress about you meeting my mother. I even thought about sneaking out without saying hello, but she saw us come in. She's not happy that I broke up with Leilani."

"Pika, you're a devil!"

"What? I just took you to church." He covered her hand with his. "Did you enjoy the service?"

"I did." Gracie allowed him to change the subject, but she was curious as to why his mother would want him to continue dating Leilani. Maybe the families were closer than Pika had let on. "I haven't been to church in a while. I enjoyed it more than I thought I would, actually. I really liked what he had to say about accepting God's love for ourselves."

Pika nodded. "Yeah, it's all good that way."

Gracie watched the beautiful landscape outside her window as they drove toward Poipu. The ocean appeared darker today as the sun skipped in and out of white puffy clouds. The trees were lush and green. Gracie saw several bright-colored chickens pecking in the light-green grasses near the roadside. "So, you said we had plans. What are they?"

"Well, not to invite myself, but what if we went back to your place and hung out on the beach? Make some lunch? Or how about a nap in that hammock you had me hang?"

"Sounds delicious," Gracie replied.

"Lunch or the nap?" Pika waggled his eyebrows.

Gracie laughed and gave him a playful slug. "Remember, I know who your mother is now."

"Oh, don't worry. I plan on behaving myself, because you haven't met my grandma yet, and she never liked Leilani."

"Really? I like your grandma already. When do I get to meet her?"

"Hmm." Pika tapped his fingers on the steering wheel. "I think soon." He pulled into the driveway of the bungalow and helped her out of the pickup. He kept hold of her hand and pulled her close to him. "You are the most beautiful woman. How did I get so lucky?"

Gracie touched his clean-shaven cheek with her fingertips. "I feel pretty lucky myself right now."

They cooked chicken breasts and vegetables with fresh pineapple on the side. Gracie enjoyed the easy way Pika moved through the kitchen. He was just as qualified to prep the food as she was, and he didn't mind cleaning up. There was a natural rhythm to their actions that made Gracie feel at ease around him. Her heart had a mind of its own, though, skipping a beat whenever Pika flashed one of his irresistible smiles.

The weather was mild enough that they decided to sit on the new patio to eat. "This is a perfect day," Gracie said. "And I think the deck and the new furniture will be better than Lexi and Derek could imagine."

Pika smiled. "Thanks. It is nice. It's fun to see the transformation, but mostly it's been nice to see you."

"Aren't you a charmer today? Trying to make up for the surprise intro to your mom?"

"You're never gonna let me live that down, are you?" Pika took a bite of chicken and leaned back in the chair.

"Never is a strong word. I wouldn't say never. Always might be more accurate."

"As in you're *always* going to give me grief about it." Pika chuckled. "At least you're honest."

Gracie gave him a smile in return but kept her thoughts to herself. *Always* indicated that she would be with Pika in the future. It meant that she would always have a chance to give him grief about his poor social skills. The thought made her smile wider and her chest flared with hope. It scared her just a tiny bit too, because she couldn't bear to think of her world without Pika in it. Time to think about something else. "Hey, I was thinking about your business idea and I wondered how serious you are, because it's a great idea."

Pika leaned forward. "I don't know. I want it to be a great idea, but what if the execution of it falls flat?"

"I bet you'd be surprised to know that you just described how I felt about certain ballets."

Pika snorted. "You lost me." He held his hand out and touched her fingertips. "But I'd like to understand."

That simple movement brought a thrill to Gracie's middle. "Well, sometimes the choreography of a certain dance seemed so complicated that I wondered if I would ever learn it. I literally felt afraid that I would fall flat on my face. But then the director—if they were good—would start breaking things down into scenes, and even into steps and suddenly, I was progressing."

"So you're saying I should stop being afraid of the big picture and look at the little things that need to happen first?"

"You read my mind."

Pika nodded. "I am afraid of stepping away from the sure thing—chopping coconuts and construction work—to take a risk that might not pay off."

"Start small. Use word of mouth and get the basic foundation of your business set up, and then keep going forward. You'll learn the steps as you go along." Gracie hesitated, watching him for a reaction. She wanted Pika to believe in himself, but she didn't want to push too hard either.

He finished the last bite of chicken and pineapple and chewed, staring off toward the ocean. "I like it. I can put a sign on the pickup while we're chopping. People could sign up to go fishing with me."

"That's brilliant! How can I help?" Gracie popped a piece of pineapple in her mouth.

"You really want to help me?" Pika studied her, as if he was worried that she would say no.

"Of course. I need something to do. Lexi and Derek won't be back for another week, and I've pretty much finished my projects here."

"Oh, I see," Pika replied. "You're just trying to find a reason to keep me coming around."

"Hey, it's not my fault if I like you."

Pika stood and pulled her up from her chair slowly. "I don't need a reason to spend time with you, Gracie. I'll be here as long as you'll let me."

"I like the sound of that," she murmured.

Pika smiled and dipped his head, kissing her slowly. He put his large hands on the small of her back and held her close to him. Gracie responded by wrapping her arms around his neck. His kisses were gentle and full of longing. With her heart beating against his, Gracie couldn't think of any place she'd rather be.

CHAPTER SIXTEEN

GRACIE

Over the next week, Gracie saw Pika every day. There was never enough time or kisses, and she'd never felt happier. They worked together on a preliminary business plan for Pika's guided tours and fishing trips. He had a lot of great ideas that were different from anything else offered through the tour companies on the island. His personal touch and detailed knowledge would be highly sought after—once they got the word out.

On Saturday, the first week of February, Gracie put the finishing touches on the house in preparation for Lexi's return. The newly married couple were flying in that day, and Lexi and Derek planned to come over later to take a look at the work that she'd done.

Pika came by to check out the house, and he brought one of Kima's woven frames. Gracie hadn't found anything that screamed at her for placement in the living room, so for now she would add another of Derek's photos in the woven frames. Pika had explained that Derek hired Kima to weave the frames so that he could sell his photos and tourists would have a ready-made souvenir.

"What do you think Lexi and Derek will say about what we've been up to while they've been gone?" Gracie said with a coy smile.

Pika returned her smile and looked around the room. "I think they will say we make a great team and maybe we should decorate another house. Oh, and they'll love the deck."

Gracie picked up a pillow from the couch and tossed it at him. "You brat."

Pika jumped up and grabbed her from the chair, tickling her until she screamed for mercy.

"Pika! I can't breathe."

"Sure, you can. You're talking." He held her hands and tickled her sides slowly.

She shrieked and tried to wriggle away. Pika held her tighter and kissed her neck below her ear. She laughed and stopped fighting him as he kissed his way up to her mouth.

He stopped by her ear and whispered, "I can't wait to see Derek's face when I kiss you."

"You'd better not, Pika Sepe!"

"Bwahahaha!" Pika laughed and tickled her again. "But you know they must have had an idea that we'd see each other. I kind of wonder if they planned for our worlds to collide."

"If so, then we really owe them." She wrapped her arms around his neck and nuzzled her face into his chest. "This has been the best couple weeks of my life."

"Fo' sho fo' me, but for you? Really?" He kissed her again. "Better than dance?"

Gracie's smile faltered and she took in a deep breath. But the thought of dance didn't bring a sharp pain of regret. Her throat relaxed, and instead of feeling like crying when she thought of all she'd left behind in her ballet career, Gracie felt peace. With a lightness in her chest, she breathed out next to Pika's skin. "Yes, better than dance. For the first time in my life, I feel like I am more than ballet. You did that for me, because you helped me see another way that I can be happy. And you definitely make me happy."

Pika shifted and scooped her in his arms. "I've never felt like this before. I love you, Gracie."

Gracie's breath caught in her throat. Her heart swelled with every good emotion she'd felt with Pika over the past couple of weeks. But those three words were so powerful. Did she have the courage to say them aloud? In one heartbeat, she felt the truth of the words before they crossed her lips. This man holding her was everything she'd ever dared dream about.

"Oh, Pika. I love you, too." She leaned forward and pressed her lips against his. His love and warmth radiated from him and she cuddled into his embrace, basking in the beauty of the moment. Pika loved her! She had found the courage to live without dance, and it felt amazing.

After a few more kisses, Gracie reminded Pika that she was supposed to help him set up social media for his new business. He muttered a complaint, but then let her go so they could get to work.

"Derek is gonna flip when he sees my business plan."

Pika's huge hand covered the mouse as he scrolled through another screen of information.

"Do you think he'll be on board to come along as a photographer?"

"After he dies of shock, yes. I've been talking about doing this for years," Pika explained. "He probably thought it was just a pipe dream."

"Or he was waiting for you to figure out that it was more than a dream," Gracie ventured.

Pika turned to her, and his gaze softened. "Why do you believe in me?"

"Why wouldn't I?"

He shrugged. "It's just...well, I worry what you'll think if this business fails."

She leaned her head on his shoulder. "Do you think any less of me that my career has essentially failed?"

"What? No." Pika put his arm around her. "You haven't failed. You were an amazing success. You're just trying something new, like me."

"I love you. I love you for trying something new and for bringing color back into my world." Gracie took a deep breath. "Whatever happens with your business, it'll be okay."

Pika chewed on his bottom lip. "I think that it's worth a shot, and hopefully, you'll be able to come help me out on some of the adventures."

"That would be wonderful!" Gracie hugged him and kissed his cheek.

Pika kissed her and moved her hair away from her face, his fingers trailing along her neck. "I gotta run so I can make it to the north shore in time to work. I'll be back tonight so I can gloat about the deck to Derek."

"Can't wait to see you."

Pika stood and pulled her up next to him. He put his face close to hers and murmured, "I'm counting down the minutes until I get to kiss you in front of Derek and Lexi." He gave her a quick peck.

"You!" Gracie smiled as he hurried out the front door. Secretly, she couldn't wait to tell Lexi all about her new boyfriend.

IT WAS ALMOST six o'clock by the time Lexi and Derek pulled into the driveway. Gracie's stomach fluttered in anticipation of showing off what she'd done. She hoped her best friend would love it. Gracie opened the door before they could knock.

There was a glow about Lexi that spoke of happiness and peace. Derek had his arm around her, and it was evident that he was more smitten than the day they were married.

"Welcome home! Did you two have a good honeymoon?"

"Gracie! It was the best!" Lexi gave her a hug. "Derek has quite the romantic streak."

"Now, don't be telling my secrets," Derek said. He gave Gracie a hug. "It's nice to see you. You look happy."

"I am," Gracie replied, laughing inwardly at the news that she and Pika would soon share.

"I can't wait to see what you've done." Lexi stepped

inside and set down her bag. "I hope you haven't been bored out of your mind while we were gone."

"Actually, I've been a lot busier than I ever imagined. This island is full of surprises." Gracie turned toward the living room. "Come and take a look."

Lexi and Derek followed her into the living room. A few seconds later, she heard Lexi gasp.

"Gracie! This is stunning. I love how you incorporated these photos into the décor." She stepped closer, admiring Derek's photography in the frames that Gracie had selected.

"Wow, I don't know what to say." Derek turned slowly around the room, a smile tugging at the corners of his mouth.

"Oh, quit being modest," Lexi said. "It looks amazing, and you know it."

They all laughed. Derek pointed at one of the photos of sea turtles kissing. "This one will always remind me of my wife."

Lexi slugged him. "Gracie remembers that story, right?" She turned toward Gracie.

"Of course. I'll never forget the Hanapepe art fair. I think you fell pretty hard that night."

"Maybe so." Lexi turned toward her husband with a soft smile. She touched another photo. "This is so fun, and it reminds me of how I fell in love with Derek."

"I think most everything around here reminds you of falling in love with Derek," Gracie teased. "But wait until you see what I've done with the bedrooms."

"Let's not wait. Show me now," Lexi demanded with a smirk.

"Yes, ma'am." Gracie marched to the first bedroom with Lexi and Derek right behind her. She opened the door and swung out her arm. "This guest bedroom has a light touch with some special features that will help anyone enjoy their stay."

Lexi walked in and admired the white quilt with elaborate stitching inside hexagons and triangles. Then she turned and noticed one of her own paintings on the wall. She sucked in a breath and put her hand over her heart, turning to Gracie with a question.

"Your paintings are inspiring, unassuming, and bring the perfect air of relaxation and rejuvenation to a room. I hope it's okay with you that I put them on display."

"Breathtaking, just like my wife," Derek said.

Lexi turned and noticed that there was a collage of her paintings on the wall above the bed. "I don't know what to say. They look so nice, but I've only ever painted for the joy of it."

"Precisely why they pull me in and light up a room so well."

Lexi pulled Gracie into a hug. "Thank you. This means so much to me."

Gracie hugged her best friend. "It means so much to me that you like it. Thank you for giving me this opportunity."

"Well, now that she's seen what you can do, she's going to keep you even busier," Derek said.

"I'm ready to work, and I want to explore every inch of this island in my spare time." Gracie stood tall and clasped her hands in front of her. "Kauai is my new home, and I'm ready to accept that."

"Gracie, you're like a different person today. What

happened while we were gone?" Lexi tilted her head, studying her friend.

That's when they heard a pounding on the door. It opened, and someone called, "Aloha?"

"Pika?" Lexi's brow furrowed. She glanced at Gracie, who couldn't hide the heat creeping up her neck.

Derek hurried out front. "Bro! What are you doing here?"

"I came by to show you the deck. Gracie didn't spoil the surprise, did she?"

"No," Gracie replied. "I haven't shown them any of your work." She hoped that he caught the double entendre she'd just thrown out.

"Oh, the deck! I almost forgot. We've been so absorbed with the interior. Have you seen what Gracie has done to this place?" Lexi asked.

Pika grinned. "She's been a busy wahine." He winked at Gracie, and she was certain that her face was red by then.

Derek opened the door and stepped out with everyone trailing behind. He and Lexi gushed over the beautifully rebuilt deck. "I love the natural stain you used. And this furniture!" Lexi turned to Pika and narrowed her eyes. "Gracie helped you pick everything out, didn't she?"

Pika chose that moment to put his arm around Gracie and pull her close. "She helped me with everything, and I helped her with everything. We make a great team." He gave her a little squeeze.

"Pika's been holding out on you guys. He has quite an eye for design," Gracie quipped.

Pika laughed and kissed Gracie's cheek. "Fo' sho."

"What in the world?" Lexi said, her mouth open in a surprised smile. "Are you two..."

"Isn't it nice how they act all surprised when they planned the whole thing?" Pika tipped his head toward Gracie.

"What do you mean?" Lexi asked, maybe a bit too innocently.

"You hired me to decorate and hired Pika to rebuild the deck at the same time. You knew we'd run into each other." Gracie tilted her head and tried to keep a straight face.

Derek slapped the table and whooped. "Pika, are you saying you actually took Gracie out on a date?"

"We've spent pretty much every day together since you guys left on your honeymoon," Gracie said. "It's been wonderful."

Lexi squealed and hugged Gracie and then Pika. "I'm so happy for you two. Gosh, you look so happy."

Pika held Gracie close to his side. "Gracie encouraged me to chase after my dreams. After kissing her, I felt like I could do anything, so I'm starting my own business for private tours of the island."

"No way!" Derek slapped Pika on the back. "Fishing, hiking, underwater photography? That biz?"

"Yeah, and I might've got my first customer today," Pika replied.

"You did?" Gracie lifted onto her tiptoes. "Pika, that's wonderful!" She kissed him and then remembered that Derek and Lexi were still there. She turned and caught Lexi's nod.

"You two just made me happier than I thought possible," Lexi said. "Coming off this honeymoon, I just want everyone to find love like we have."

"Lex, don't get carried away. They've only been on a few dates," Derek warned.

"Nah, she's cool." Pika fist-bumped Derek.

Lexi gave Gracie a look that held a million questions, but she just smiled at her friend. There would be time to talk later. For the moment, she stayed tucked tight to Pika's side, enjoying the feeling of belonging he gave her. Derek and Pika were talking about his business ideas, and Lexi jumped in with questions. Soon, the budding romance was out of the main spotlight and the four friends were brainstorming how to make Pika's dream a reality.

CHAPTER SEVENTEEN

GRACIE

On Sunday, Lexi and Derek accompanied Pika and Gracie to church. They arrived early enough to find a pew where they could all sit together during the service, including Kima. She seemed much more friendly to Lexi than she had to Gracie the week before.

"Just give her time to get used to the idea," Pika whispered. "I still need to introduce you to my grandma. You will love her, and I know she'll love you."

"When do you think you'll let me meet her?"

"Let's go see her this week, okay?"

Gracie nodded. During the sermon, she glanced around the congregation, but she didn't see Brave Kamai anywhere. If any other family members were there, Pika didn't mention it. After services, Pika had to work, so Gracie ended up having lunch with Lexi and Derek. They asked her for more details about dating Pika, and she told them that it was really the most mundane tasks and work that had brought them together.

"Speaking of mundane," Derek said, "I have to cut out for about an hour to get things in line for tomorrow." He kissed Lexi and waved at Gracie.

Lexi watched him leave the room, a contented smile on her face. Then she turned to Gracie. "Let's walk outside to the beach."

The two friends walked along the shore, chatting about the beauty of the day. Lexi looked out toward the ocean and then got a mischievous gleam in her eye. "So is Pika a good kisser?"

"Lexi!"

"What? I bet he is, huh?"

Gracie giggled. "Fo' sho."

They both laughed. Gracie ventured closer to the waves lapping the shore. Her feet sank partway in the wet sand. "It's like a postcard here. I have to keep reminding myself that it's real."

"I felt the same way when I moved here," Lexi replied. "Hey, Derek and I want to go out to dinner with you and Pika—our treat."

"Sure, where would you like to go?"

"Beach House Restaurant."

Gracie's eyes widened. She'd looked up the menu online before, and the photos of the food looked almost too good to eat. The price tag on the plates made it so the food was impossible for her to eat—at least, her budget made it impossible.

"Don't give me that look," Lexi said playfully. "I need an excuse to drag Derek away from his work."

"So he's keeping pretty busy?" Gracie asked.

Lexi grinned and her eyes sparkled with happiness. "He is, and I'm so proud of him. It's what he's always dreamed of."

"You're both living your dreams, aren't you?"

"It feels that way right now," Lexi replied. "I know that we'll face other hard things, but I feel confident that we'll be able to get through them together."

"I'm happy for you." Gracie bumped Lexi's hip. "You deserve as much happiness as you can handle." And she meant what she said. After her friend had lost her parents in the car accident, Gracie had seen how trauma had the power to change a person's life. Thankfully, Lexi's north star kept guiding her toward good things. She worked harder than anyone Gracie knew, and in part, she hid herself in that work to cope with the loss of her parents. Lexi's brother, Jordan, did the same thing, and the two had leaned on each other to get through those awful years of grieving.

It reminded Gracie of losing her mother too soon, so long ago. Her father had remarried a nice woman, but he'd focused on her children and Gracie hadn't developed the close relationship with her father that she might have liked. Ballet had become her family, her foundation, her very breath. It was beautiful and dangerous at the same time to depend on something so much for life's joy. Thankfully, Lexi had given her a chance to rediscover life, and it turned out that Pika was her guiding star. Gracie sighed.

"You are so whipped," Lexi said with a laugh. "I love seeing you this way."

"It feels amazing. I love him, you know."

"You do?" Lexi pressed her lips together as if to hold in an excited squeal. "Have you told him?"

"Yes, right after he told me."

"Gracie!" Lexi did squeal then and jumped up and down, hugging her friend. Then she paused and fanned herself with her hands. "Okay, I promise not to get too carried away. It's just that ever since last year, I've thought that you and Pika belonged together. It's been so hard to wait for you two to figure it out."

Gracie shook her head. "You're the best friend a girl could ever have. Thanks for providing the opportunity for me to find happiness."

"Of course. Now let's get on the phone and make some reservations for Tuesday night."

PIKA PICKED Gracie up from Lexi's house after work and drove her home. She rolled her window down halfway and let the warm breeze caress her as they traveled toward Poipu. He was tired from work, but excited because he was taking a couple tourists fishing the next morning.

"It's really happening." Gracie squeezed his hand.

Pika nodded. "Let's hope they don't get too seasick."

"Oh yeah, I forgot about that. I was lucky in that regard."

"Don't worry. I gave them some instructions to help. It should be great." He pulled up to the house and hopped out to grab her door.

"Do you want to come in?" Gracie asked as he walked her toward the front door.

"I'd better not. I have an early day tomorrow and you're a little too irresistible, but I would like a few kisses." He smiled and put his arms around her.

"I think I can spare a few for my favorite person." She tipped her head back and met his lips. He kissed her soft and slow, until her insides melted and her legs felt like they would sink into the sand beneath her feet.

"I love you, my beautiful wahine," Pika murmured. "Want to get together for lunch tomorrow?"

Gracie recognized the Hawaiian word for woman and smiled. "I would love that. I'll make something. See you around noon?"

"I can't wait." Pika kissed her again and then turned to go.

Gracie watched him get in his beat-up pickup and drive away. She couldn't stop smiling, and it was the best feeling ever.

CHAPTER EIGHTEEN

GRACIE

The next morning, Gracie woke early and grabbed a couple of canvas shopping bags. She planned to hit the farmer's market to purchase fresh produce for the week. The pineapple was better than candy. Gracie had been trying several Hawaiian recipes under Pika's tutelage.

The farmer's market wasn't crowded, but there were still plenty of customers. Gracie chose two pineapples and several fresh vegetables. She carried her purchases into another tent that sold fresh herbs. She spotted a pile of bright yellow lemons and grabbed a few. Pika had told her he'd bring fish home that they could fry for supper. Gracie paid for the citrus fruits and turned to leave the tent, but a woman was blocking her way.

"Excuse me," Gracie said softly, turning to walk the other direction.

"Wait, you're Gracie, aren't you?" The woman was

Hawaiian with glossy dark hair that fell in ringlets to her waist. Her eyes were light-colored and almond-shaped, and when she smiled, Gracie thought she was beautiful—until the smile turned dangerous.

"Yes, and you are?"

"I'm Leilani Kamai. Pika's fiancée." She put her hand on her hip and stared at Gracie.

Swallowing, Gracie tried to find the right words to say. This was the woman Pika had warned her about—the woman who didn't want to take no for an answer. "Pika Sepe?"

"Yes, my Pika Sepe," she replied.

"I've been dating Pika for over two weeks and—"

"Pika and I have been promised to one another for years," Leilani interrupted.

"No, he told me that he broke up with you," Gracie protested.

Leilani shook her head and laughed. "You poor thing. Pika is a gentle soul. He has a hard time telling people no. He didn't want to hurt your feelings when he saw how hard you'd fallen for him. What was it he said? Oh, something about feeling sorry for you because your ballet career was over. *Such a nice girl. I'm just trying to help her through the hard times.*"

Gracie sucked in a breath. "It's not true," she whispered. "You don't know what you're saying." A thread of doubt wound its way around her heart. How did Leilani know about her ballet career? Had Brave been spying on her? Gracie shook her head. That was crazy. "It's not true."

"No, *you* don't know what you're saying." Leilani stood. "You don't know me. Pika is mine. He is in love with me.

Yes, he likes to kiss beautiful women and he's pretty good at it, but at the end of the day, he always comes back to me. You need to go back to the mainland and quit messing with things you don't know anything about."

"Stop! I don't believe you!" Gracie said, her voice rising. She held her bags tight and ran for the door.

"You should believe me! There is no place for you in Pika's life or on this island!" Leilani yelled after her.

Gracie ran down the road, gasping for breath as a river of tears poured down her face. It couldn't be true. It wasn't true. Pika had said that Leilani wouldn't accept the fact that they were over. He had broken up with her, hadn't he? Gracie needed Pika. He would sort out this mess and straighten Leilani out, because if he didn't, that awful woman might be right—there was no place on the island for Gracie without him.

GRACIE WIPED her eyes and drove home, breathing in and out slowly. It was a misunderstanding. Leilani was crazy— that was it. Pika had said she wanted to marry him and he'd broken up with her. Gracie's heart hammered with worry. What if Pika hadn't been truthful with her? She grabbed her cell phone, about to call Pika, but then thought better of it. He wouldn't be able to talk to her while he was fishing, and she didn't want to interrupt his first expedition.

By the time Gracie returned to the house, she'd talked herself out of fifteen percent of the worry. She unloaded the groceries and told herself to be patient. She would see Pika in a few hours.

The phone rang and Gracie jumped, and then she scolded herself for her nerves. She flipped the phone over and saw the number of her agent and almost dropped the phone.

"Andrew?" she answered with a squeak in her voice.

"Gracie! I have the best news. Are you sitting down?" His voice boomed over the phone as if he weren't an ocean away.

She backed against the living room chair and sank down. "What kind of news?"

"The Tchaikovsky kind of news." Andrew paused. "Odette. Gracie, they want you to audition again for Odette."

"What? Andrew, what are you talking about? I tried for that part. Is this another company? I'm retired. How could anyone want me to audition?"

"It's New York City Ballet. The lead tore her Achilles in an accident. They contacted several ballerinas who have performed the role and previously auditioned for the part, and they've only come up with a couple who can audition. Gracie, if you want this part, it's yours. You have so much more experience than these other girls."

"Wait, you remember I'm in Kauai, right?" Gracie rubbed her forehead, trying to sort through the stream of information.

"Yes, yes, and they understand that means you can't be here tomorrow, but if you could get here by Friday—oh, that's February 14th. Are you ready to be the sweetheart of ballet again?"

"But Andrew, I don't know if I can. I'm out of shape."

"Gracie, you followed the doctor's orders and you've

taken time off to rest. Remember your doctor said you could try again and see what happens? You have the chance to leave the stage in a lead role that every ballerina dreams of. You can do this. The trainers can help you get through it if it's what you want."

Gracie hesitated. How was this even happening? She had closed that chapter of her life. "Andrew, I don't know."

"Don't answer right now. Think about it today. Book a flight just in case and call me later, okay?"

Gracie looked up at the ceiling. There was so much enthusiasm in Andrew's voice. All the emotions swirling inside her made it hard to think. "Okay, I'll consider it, but please don't give any promises or even a flicker of hope to anyone. I really don't think I can do this."

"But you'll think about it, right?"

"Yes."

"I'll talk to you later." Andrew ended the call before she could say anything else.

She stared at the phone in her hand, gripping it until her fingertips turned white. Why was this happening now? She'd barely accepted her fate, and now it was as if her pointe shoes were being dangled in front of her—taunting her. Gracie walked into her bedroom and dropped her phone on the counter. She moved across the tile floor in several simple steps, arching her back, lifting onto her toes, and twirling around. It was a familiar warm-up, and it didn't cause any pain. If anything, it made her feel more awake and alive. The ritual she'd performed for so many years jump-started her brain into dance mode.

With a kick of her toes, she pointed her left leg and right, watching the tendons flex in her feet and ankles. How much would she be able to practice or perform before everything flared up again and became painful? Even though Andrew had told her to think about it, she knew the answer her heart wanted to make. Her heart chose Pika. He made her heart dance.

She didn't want to leave the island when she was just starting to find her place among the lush tropical paradise. For a moment, she wondered about the part in the ballet. Perhaps she could take the role, perform, and then retire?

Gracie sank back into the chair that looked out the picture windows of the living room. She hadn't been thinking straight ever since her run-in with Leilani. She clenched her fists when she thought of the encounter. It was nearly time for Pika to arrive. She would talk to him, and everything would make sense. All the confusion in her mind would fall away when he kissed her and told her how much he loved her.

Gracie hurried out to the front entryway and opened the door. She didn't want to think about ballet or ex-girlfriends. Pika was coming, and she wanted to greet him with a smile. While she waited for him to arrive, she walked around the property admiring the lush trees and blooming flowers. The island had been a haven for her, and now it was hard to imagine leaving.

A honk signaled Pika's arrival, and Gracie hurried around front to meet him.

"Aloha!" He jumped out of his pickup and wrapped his big arms around her.

"I take it things went well?" Gracie's voice was muffled against his chest.

Pika kissed her. "I am so glad to see you. And yes, it was

awesome. They tipped me fifty bucks!"

"What? Really?" Gracie felt her chest warm. Pika's enthusiasm was infectious. He looked like a boy who had just caught the biggest fish.

"Yeah, and I used your idea to encourage them to leave reviews on our site and share with friends. They said they would for sure." Pika walked back over to his pickup as he talked. He reached into the back and pulled out the long, flat blade of his machete. "I need to wash the fish guts off my machete. I probably need to stop by my house and sharpen it before I go up to Ke'e today." He took it around the back of the house and used the hose and a rag to wash it off. He set it down and stretched his arms over his head. "It was amazing today. The fish were after us and the water was perfect."

Gracie listened to him talk. He was so excited. She'd never seen him quite like this before. It was fun to see this side of Pika. She thought about what Leilani had said and dismissed it. Gracie felt foolish for listening to that crazy woman. Anyone could see that Pika loved her. He was here with her, not Leilani.

The chance to play Odette in that fabulous ballet was still pretty exciting, but Gracie didn't want to kill Pika's mood. She was seventy-five percent sure that she would turn down the role, and for that reason, she didn't want to tell anyone in case they might sway her one direction or the other. It felt important that she make this decision on her own.

"I'm happy that you're happy. Tell me about the fish you caught." Gracie followed Pika as he walked back around the house talking nonstop about his fishing expedition.

CHAPTER NINETEEN

PIKA

*P*ika couldn't find the words to explain how different he felt, but he didn't need to explain to Gracie. She understood because she had encouraged him to follow his dreams. It was happiness and excitement and pride all mixed together creating a feeling that made him smile bigger than he had in years. He had done something today that he'd dreamed about for years, something that other people had warned him not to try. And he'd done it because of Gracie. He was overflowing with excitement to tell her every detail of how his first hired fishing tour had gone.

She listened intently, and Pika fell in love with her even more. God was smiling on him, because how else could Pika have found this gorgeous, talented, smart woman who was interested in him and his life?

They ate lunch together, and Gracie asked him questions about what his next steps were.

"Derek said he'd help by taking some photos of me fishing and other stuff so we'll have more pictures to post online."

"That's a great idea, and it serves a double purpose, because it will tie Derek into those excursions that include photography."

"See, you are always coming up with great ideas." Pika leaned over and kissed Gracie's cheek. "How do you do it?"

Gracie smiled. "Maybe I've spent too much time around Lexi. She's the ultimate businesswoman."

"Ha, either way, I think you're perfect."

"Thank you." Her cheeks turned a little pink, and that made him want to kiss her more, but he kept hearing something. "I hear chimes ringing from your bedroom. Is that your phone?"

Gracie patted her pocket. "Oh, I must have left it on the bathroom counter. Hang on."

A couple minutes later, she came out of the bedroom looking slightly flustered.

"Are you okay?"

"Me? Sure. Why do you ask?"

"I don't know. You seem a little anxious." Pika watched her carefully for any reaction.

Her face relaxed and she smiled with what Pika had come to recognize as her stage smile. The flashing of her white teeth appeared to be a smile, but her eyes held the real truth. Gracie had told him once that she had danced an entire movement with a sprained elbow, smiling and blinking back the tears. She was an excellent dancer with acting skills to call on when needed.

"Oh, I had left some messages about the garden area out there, and I'm not making much headway. Don't worry." She smiled, but then she looked out the window at the ocean.

Whatever was bothering her, she wasn't going to tell him. He wished she trusted him enough to share what was on her mind. With a breath, he relaxed his shoulders. The important thing was that he trusted her. Gracie was genuine. She wasn't going to hurt him, and this wasn't just an island fling. She had said she wanted to live in Kauai, on the island, forever. She wanted to be with him. He smiled and pulled Gracie in for a hug. "I love you," he murmured.

"Oh, Pika." Her voice was soft and she wound her hands around his neck, pulling him closer. She brushed her lips over his and clung to him tightly as they kissed.

"I'm here for you," Pika whispered, "whenever you want to tell me what's on your mind."

GRACIE WANTED TO BELIEVE HIM, but her heart was tender, and her feelings were still bruised from Leilani's emotional beating. And when she had gone to get her phone, there were three texts from Andrew with more details about the audition.

The part of Odette is yours, if you want it, the last text had said.

When Gracie read it, her heart had jumped up into her throat, and no matter how many times she swallowed, she couldn't get it back down into her chest. She just needed time to figure out her decision. Pika was there waiting and looking worried. Gracie took a breath, and instead of giving her heart to Pika, she hesitated. If she told him that she didn't want to take the part because she didn't want to leave him, would he encourage her to go anyway? She worried that she might not survive the aftermath if she admitted how madly in love she was with him and he didn't feel the same way.

"Thank you for being here," she whispered back. "Will I see you again tonight?"

"Are there fish in that ocean?" Pika chuckled.

Gracie laughed. "I guess that's a yes."

"No guessing about it. How about I call you as soon as I get off work?"

"Oh my goodness!" Gracie put a hand to her forehead. "I almost forgot to tell you that we have reservations tomorrow night with Lexi and Derek at Beach House Restaurant!"

"Well, you didn't forget, so I guess that means I'd better go by my house to make sure I have something decent to wear. Might have to beg my mother for laundry help."

Gracie shook her head. "Okay, I'll let you go, then."

Pika kissed her and hurried to jump in his pickup.

Gracie cleaned up the kitchen and was just rinsing out the sink when she remembered his machete. She hurried around back and looked for the blade by the hose, but it was gone. He had remembered his tool. Part of her was disappointed because she would have gladly followed him to deliver the machete to his house. Gracie smiled. It would have been a perfect opportunity to steal a couple kisses while she was at it, but she would have to wait until tomorrow.

She felt a small twinge of guilt because she hadn't told Pika about the ballet audition or about Leilani. If she was honest about the ballet opportunity, it was the one role that could tempt her out of retirement, but she wasn't sure it was the best decision for her. Part of her worried that if she stepped back onstage, she wouldn't be able to leave gracefully again. There would always be some role that she could get by, until her body deteriorated to the point of pain and scarring that no amount of physical therapy could treat.

Gracie rolled up the hose and walked along the sandy beach that was her backyard. She tried to listen to her heart, but all she could hear was the ocean waves rolling in, never ceasing, always moving.

CHAPTER TWENTY

PIKA

Pika pulled into his driveway and rushed inside to sort through the pile of clean laundry that had been sitting on his couch for two days. He pulled out a slightly rumpled shirt, white with dark blue plumeria flowers printed on the fabric, and shook it out. It would have to do. He hauled the rest of the clothes into his bedroom, and when he came out, Leilani was standing in his living room.

He stopped and raised his eyebrows. "Um, hey?"

Leilani crossed the living room to stand in front of him. "Pika, I've missed you so much. I came to talk to you because I found out that you're making a huge mistake."

Pika rolled his eyes. "Lei, I don't have time for this. I have to get to work."

"She doesn't love you, Pika. Don't be stupid. Can't you see what she's doing?"

"What are you talking about?"

"Your new girlfriend, Gracie," Leilani spat. "I know all about her, but it's sad that you don't. You're her distraction from her broken career. As soon as she finds another part to dance, she'll be gone."

"Whoa, you'd better watch your mouth." Pika let his voice rise in a way that Leilani had probably never heard. "You don't know anything about Gracie, if that's what you think."

Leilani flinched for half a second, and Pika thought maybe he'd made an impact. Then she took a breath and another step closer. "Listen to me. She's looking for an island fling. Tourists want stories and adventures to go home with them. Don't be her escapade. What does she even know about you? Does she know you chop coconuts for a living?" Leilani grabbed his hand and turned it over, running her fingers over the hard calluses on his palms. "Is she interested in someone who holds a machete all day?"

Pika shook his head. "What do you mean?"

Leilani continued as if she were reading a script. "Because I am. I know you, and I don't mind your job."

He pulled his hand back. "Yes, she knows, and she loves me anyway."

Leilani reached her arms around his neck, and before Pika could react, she kissed him. He pulled back, but Leilani hung onto him and continued kissing him.

"Stop!" Pika pushed her away. "What are you doing?"

"I'm kissing my boyfriend." Leilani smiled and took another step forward.

"Get out!" Pika yelled. "Don't touch me. Don't walk a

foot in the house, and don't ever approach me or Gracie again."

"Pika! Get control of yourself," Leilani retorted.

His hands were in tight fists and his breathing was rapid. "Get. Out. Or I will call the police and have you removed."

Leilani's eyes widened and she sniffed. "I don't know what has gotten into you, Pika Sepe." She walked past him and onto his front step. "Such a waste," she muttered as she walked across his yard.

The rage Pika felt was giving way to fear. He put his hands over his face. What had Leilani done? How could he allow her to kiss him in his own home? His mind immediately supplied the answer, that Leilani was conniving and a little bit crazy, but still, he should have known better. Pika growled and gathered up his stuff to go to work. There would be time to sort things out in his head later. For now, Leilani better have taken his message to heart.

THE NEXT DAY, Pika was out on the ocean at seven in the morning. He had worked late the night before and part of him knew he was avoiding Gracie. He just couldn't face her after what happened with Leilani. Exhaustion had finally taken over his guilt, but he still wanted to talk to Gracie about what had happened. He owed it to her, even if no one else knew.

He struggled to stay focused on his three clients and keep an enthusiastic smile for them as he guided their fishing efforts. Luckily, a ninety-pound blue marlin on the line made up for anything Pika might have been lacking.

His client, a man in his fifties, was so excited about the fish that he tipped Pika fifty dollars.

By the time they made it to shore, Pika felt like the day had turned around. He grinned as he helped his customers, took pictures, and then cleaned up around his boat. He was bending over his fishing gear when he felt a tingle across the back of his neck. He looked up and caught sight of Leilani on the dock. She wasn't looking at him, instead she smiled at his clients as they made their way down the dock. Pika felt his chest expand with anger. He didn't want to lose his temper in public. He didn't even want to see Leilani. He looked her way again, wondering what plan she had today.

CHAPTER TWENTY-ONE

GRACIE

Gracie sang along to the upbeat Hawaiian music as she approached the docks where Pika would be cleaning up his boat. The cooler on the seat next to her carried two piña colada smoothies, fresh-cut pineapple, and blueberry muffins. It would be fun to surprise him with brunch. Pika had started the day well before seven, so he would certainly be hungry by the time he finished up with his clients.

A few people milled around the docks, mostly other fishermen cleaning and prepping their boats for the next trip out to the vast ocean. Gracie stepped out of her car and began walking across the lot to the edge of the dock. She was halfway there when she noticed Leilani leaning against a palm tree. Gracie paused and narrowed her eyes. Leilani watched Pika closely, but he didn't seem to even know she was there. In order to get to Pika, Gracie would have to pass by Leilani. She took a deep breath and squared her shoulders, determined to ignore the ex-girlfriend. Leilani was so intent in her stare-down of Pika that she didn't notice Gracie and Gracie didn't look back once she'd walked past her.

Pika looked up as Gracie approached and his face split into a wide smile.

"You're the most beautiful thing I've seen today." He stood and brushed his hands on his shorts.

"Good morning to you, too," Gracie replied. "I brought you something to eat."

Pika embraced her and kissed her softly. "You did, huh?" He glanced down at her hands and back up to her face. "I don't see anything. Does that mean you're the treat?"

Gracie swatted Pika's arm and giggled as he nuzzled her neck. "I left it in the car. I can help you here if you need it."

"Thank you. What did I do to deserve you?" He motioned to the boat. "I just need to mop up. Would you like to wipe down the seats?"

Gracie nodded. Pika tossed her a towel and they climbed aboard his boat. When she looked back toward the palm tree, Leilani was gone. Gracie scanned the beach and didn't see any sign of her. She focused on cleaning the boat with Pika and was easily distracted by his happy reports of the morning's fishing expedition.

Twenty minutes later, they sat on the beach and enjoyed brunch. Gracie dug her hand into the sand and let it filter through her fingertips. "What do you have planned the rest of the day?"

"I'm going to take the early shift chopping at Ke'e and

then I'll come home and get ready to take a beautiful girl out to dinner at Beach House."

"You remembered." Gracie kissed his cheek.

"How could I forget? It's what will get me through the day today."

Gracie smiled and then she saw a woman who reminded her of Leilani. She leaned forward, but after a moment realized she had been mistaken.

"What is it?" Pika tried to follow her gaze.

"I saw Leilani here on the dock when I arrived this morning."

Pika groaned and shook his head. "Have I told you she's lolo?"

Gracie chuckled. "A couple times, but she seems a little more than crazy. Did you see her?"

"Yes." Pika nodded. "But I ignored her. I don't know what she was doing." He leaned back on his hands and blew out a breath of air. "When I went to my house between jobs yesterday, she showed up."

Gracie turned to look at Pika. "What?"

"I walked into my bedroom to put away laundry and when I came back she was standing in my living room. She started going on about how I was making a mistake dating you and then she—well, she kissed me." Pika frowned and looked at Gracie. "I yelled at her and told her to get out or I would call the cops."

For a second, Gracie couldn't catch her breath. "She kissed you? How does that even—"

"I know, it sounds bad. I promise I didn't kiss her back. She is not my girlfriend. You are." Pika leaned forward and put his arm around Gracie.

She could imagine Leilani kissing Pika, but she also knew how strong he was. Pika was tall and muscular. It would be hard to kiss him if he didn't want to. Thoughts collided in Gracie's mind and suddenly she felt small and hurt. She shrugged out from under his arm and stood, brushing off her shorts.

"Gracie? I'm sorry. I wanted to tell you, but maybe that was the wrong thing?" Pika stood next to her and gathered up her things, putting them back in the cooler.

"No, I'm glad you were honest, but I can't understand how you could let her kiss you."

"I didn't want her to kiss me. I told her I didn't want her to come around ever again," Pika replied.

"Then what was she doing here this morning?" Gracie motioned to the tree where Leilani had stood earlier.

"I don't know." Pika groaned and pushed his hand through his hair. "I didn't talk to her. She's part of my past, and I do care for her, but with the way she's acting now I don't think we can even be friends."

It seemed that everything Pika said just made Gracie feel worse. She didn't want to think about his past, his ex-girlfriend who was still crazy in love with him. She didn't want to think about how she was the island misfit. "I think I need some space." Gracie bent and picked up the cooler. "I'll talk to you later."

"What? No, don't go. Gracie, I'm sorry. What can I do to make this right?" Pika took hold of her arm.

She felt the strength in his arms and again the question of how Leilani ever got close enough to kiss him spun through her mind. Gracie looked pointedly at his hand and Pika immediately let go of her arm.

"I'm sorry. Please don't go," he said quietly.

"I have to," Gracie murmured and jogged toward her car.

Gracie caught a glimpse of Pika in her rearview mirror, trying to chase her down as she pulled out of the lot. There were no words to describe what was happening inside her mind and body at that moment. Gracie searched for breath, and still it took everything she had to draw in a ragged mouthful of too-humid air. She made herself take another breath, and then she cried out, unable to hold in the pain. Every doubt she'd experienced about her relationship with Pika rained down on her like an angry storm.

Nothing made sense. What was real and what was imagined? She wanted to believe him when he spoke about Leilani in the past, but the woman was clearly determined to disrupt their relationship. Leilani claimed that Pika still loved her and then a few days later she kissed him in his own house.

How could Pika have been faking everything? The way he looked at her—the way he had just kissed her and professed his love—how could someone pretend like that? Tears ran down her face, and Gracie let them fall. Nothing mattered now. It was all a lie. Her life was a lie. She had come to Kauai trying to start over, but she'd been fooling herself all along. Her life was nothing without ballet. And that was when she knew she had to accept the part to play Odette. She would return to the stage, to her life, and she would make it work for as long as she could.

Her phone rang, and Gracie glanced down at the console to see a picture of her and Pika together on the screen. A hard lump of tears choked off her breath as she grappled for the phone, dismissing the call and turning it off. Of course he would call and try to explain everything, but it didn't matter now. Whatever his reasons, Leilani was right: Gracie didn't belong on the island. It was time to go home.

She didn't go back to the bungalow, because if Pika wanted to talk to her, he would surely show up at the place where they had fallen in love. Gracie gripped the steering wheel and drove carefully past the neighborhood where she'd thought she was starting a new life. She drove down to the beach and parked her car on the roadside. It was difficult to slow her breathing, but she closed her eyes and focused on the erratic beats of her heart, willing it to slow down. When her voice was steady, she would contact Andrew and let him know that she would be in New York City by Friday for the audition.

Red-eye flights left every night for the mainland. Maybe there was even time to catch a plane tonight. Gracie powered her phone back on and found a site to purchase tickets out of Lihue Airport. There might be standby tickets, but as her breathing slowed, she tried to think more sensibly. She couldn't leave without talking to Lexi. More tears streamed down her cheeks when she thought of leaving her best friend behind. They had so many great plans in the works, but Gracie couldn't work for Burke's Higher Steps with a broken heart.

She found a flight leaving Tuesday, the following night, with a seat available, and she booked a ticket. One day. That was all she had left on this island. The tears kept coming, and Gracie wiped her eyes, clearing her vision so she could see to drive to Lexi's house. Everything felt numb. That seemed to be the only way to get the tears to stop—to stop feeling.

It worked for a few minutes, but once Lexi opened the door, Gracie fell apart again. It took a few minutes for her to get the story out through the sobs that shook her body.

Lexi listened and put her arms around her. "There must be some misunderstanding. That can't be what Pika wanted. He loves you."

"He was kissing her," Gracie cried.

Lexi pressed her lips together. "Was he kissing her? Or was she kissing him?"

"Does it really matter?" Gracie leaned her head back on the couch. "She was in his house kissing him. That doesn't just happen."

"Gracie, it just doesn't feel right. I'm so sorry."

"That's because it isn't right. I love him. This hurts so much."

"I remember how I felt when I thought I'd lost Derek. That was a misunderstanding too, remember?" Lexi leaned forward to look in Gracie's eyes.

She shook her head. "A different kind of misunderstanding that didn't involve Derek kissing another woman. It's over. My life as I knew it is completely over. Fighting it is just making me feel worse."

"Gracie, your life is not over," Lexi soothed.

"My life on this island is over." Gracie sniffed. "I know this will be hard for you to hear. And I know you might want to talk me out of it, but Andrew called me today."

"Your agent? Why would he call you?"

"Because he wanted to tell me that there is a desperate need for a seasoned ballerina to play the part of Odette in

Swan Lake. In New York City. Their lead had an injury, and he basically told me that I had the part if I wanted to take it."

"Isn't that the role you auditioned for before coming here?" Lexi covered her mouth and shook her head.

Gracie nodded.

"But Gracie, you said the doctor told you not to dance anymore. You've been building a new life here, and you have so many possibilities. Please don't give up now."

"The doctor said I needed to rest before considering performing again. I've done that." Gracie hugged her knees to her chest and rested her chin on top of her knees. "I didn't tell Pika about the offer, because I wanted to think about it and make the decision without anybody else's opinion influencing me. But I think I've been kidding myself that I could just walk away from ballet and still feel whole. I booked a flight. I'm leaving tomorrow night."

"No! That's too soon. Please don't go," Lexi argued.

"I have to do this. Andrew said I had to be there by Valentine's Day in order to audition for the part. I know it's a risk, but I also know how to be careful. I want to do this, and I want to see what other opportunities I have. Maybe I can teach dance even if I can't perform onstage."

"Is that what you want? Do you want to teach dance?" Lexi asked.

"I've thought about it before. I've thought about how I could impact other girls' lives the way mine was, and that it might be fun to teach someone about something that I love so much."

"Gracie, you could totally do that anywhere that you wanted. Even here."

She shook her head. There were too many emotions leaking out from her eyes and her heart. She didn't know if she could trust the truth anymore when reality had smacked her so hard in the face. She'd thought she'd known what she was doing on the island, but Leilani had changed all of that. "I can't do it, Lexi. I don't want to see Pika. If I see him, then I'll talk myself into staying here, and I just don't belong."

"So you're going to run away rather than risk a chance at love that could change your life?"

Gracie stood and walked over to the window. Anger bubbled up in her chest. "I already took a huge risk. I let myself fall in love, and look at me now. It's too hard. I've been through too much."

Lexi sat cross-legged on the floor and watched Gracie with a sad expression. "I'm sorry you feel that way. Is there anything I can do that would help you? Is there any way that I could convince you to stay and try a little longer?"

Gracie looked out the window at the beach with the waves rolling in softly. The white surf crested the tips of the waves, making the whirring sound that she'd already grown accustomed to. "Just let me go."

She heard a sniff and looked over to see tears running down Lexi's cheeks.

Gracie hurried over to sit next to her friend and put her arms around her. "I'm sorry. This isn't at all what I planned for my life. I'm just trying to salvage what's left."

Lexi wiped her cheek and nodded. "This isn't what I planned for my life either, but I'm telling you, Gracie, it's the best decision I ever made. It was hard to do, but I changed everything. I'm so happy now. Sometimes we have to go through really hard things to find the good. I wish it wasn't that way."

Lexi was trying to cheer her up, but that empty feeling in Gracie's heart made it so all those comforting words just bounced off. In truth, she didn't want to feel better. She wanted to be sad, brokenhearted, and angry at Pika and at the world. "Thanks for understanding. And don't worry. When I finish the ballet, I will come back and visit you."

Lexi hugged her. "Give me all the details. Derek and I will come and see you perform."

Fresh tears ran down Gracie's face. "I'd better go and get packed."

"Do you want some help?"

"No, I need a little time alone."

"Will you please talk to Pika? I still think that there's more to this than we can imagine. Don't fly thousands of miles without talking to him first."

Gracie lifted her left shoulder and let it drop. "I'll think about it."

As she drove away from Lexi's house, her mind was made up. So what if Pika could explain away the kiss from his ex-girlfriend? The event had been the catalyst Gracie needed to self-check what was going on in her life. It was time to quit pretending that she was someone who walked through life instead of danced.

CHAPTER TWENTY-TWO

PIKA

Pika drove to Gracie's house, but she wasn't there. He waited an hour, trying to call her, before he finally gave up and drove to the north shore to chop coconuts with Jefe. He tried calling Derek on the way but couldn't get through to him either.

He was so mad at Leilani that he chopped ten coconuts before Jefe stopped him and told him to pay attention to how many customers they had.

"Sorry, bro. I've had a rough day."

"I can see that. Woman problems?"

Pika snorted. "You could say that." A few more customers came up to the bed of Jefe's pickup then, so Pika went back to work. He had too much time to think. Part of him wondered if Leilani had been telling the truth. He shook his head. That didn't make sense, except that some of the things Leilani said had cut him to the core. They were the very things that Pika had been worrying over. It was probably better to accept the truth—he chopped coconuts for a living. Why would a famous ballerina be interested in him?

The hours passed, and Pika focused on the methodical swing of his machete. Somehow, he made it through, and he drove straight from the beach to his grandmother's house.

"Hey, Tutu," he called as he entered her house. "You are a sight for sore eyes."

"What's that supposed to mean? I know I'm old, but do I look that bad?" Grandma cackled.

Pika smiled and kissed her cheek. "I've had a pretty bad day." He had come to his grandma instead of his mother because he feared that his mother would tell him that his doubts about Gracie were correct.

"Well, come sit down and tell me about it."

Pika sat down and spilled his guts. He told his grandmother about Leilani and how she'd ruined everything. And then he admitted his doubts. "I keep thinking about how easily Leilani was able to fool Gracie. Maybe she didn't love me after all if she has so little trust in me."

"Coconuts! You've been chopping too many coconuts!"

"But she won't even talk to me," Pika protested.

"You're smarter than this, Pika. That girl loves you. When has she ever looked at you with anything but awe and wonder in her eyes?"

"But how did you ...?"

"I've seen you two together." Grandma sat up straighter. "You may think I never leave this house, but with all the stars in your eyes, you could walk right by your own mother and not even notice. *Everyone* has seen you with Gracie, and it's obvious the two of you are smitten."

Pika sat back and thought about those words. If everyone had seen him with Gracie, then it meant that most of the Kamai family would have seen him. How many meddling brothers and sisters would it have taken to help Leilani come up with her plan? He shook his head. It didn't seem like Brave or Lenora to go to such lengths. He stopped himself from placing the blame on his longtime friends.

"Do you love her?" Grandma's voice was softer now.

"I do. She is the most amazing woman. I don't know if I'm good enough for her, but I want to be."

"There you go. Now that's true love, my boy." Gran patted his knee. "Don't let her go. Do whatever it takes to find her and explain what happened, but more importantly to explain how much you love her."

"But how do I do that when she won't speak to me?"

Gran frowned. "Get your friends involved. Write a letter, leave a message ... anything is better than what's happening now, right?"

Pika felt the urgency of what his grandmother was speaking of. He needed to do something before it was too late. "You are right, as usual. Thanks, Tutu. I'm going to go make a fool of myself."

"Not a fool. Go, but if I see Leilani anywhere, my walking stick might have a mind of its own."

Pika chuckled. "I'll let you know what happens." He hugged his grandmother and hurried out the door. The first thing he would do was drive to Derek and Lexi's house and see if they could help him find Gracie.

As he drove along the winding highway, he thought about what Leilani had said earlier that afternoon: she didn't mind his job. The dig was subtle, but it was there. Like his job wasn't good enough. The truth was that Leilani did mind his job. She'd made enough comments for him to understand that she didn't think it was a good career choice. It was so different from Gracie, who had asked him about his dreams and ambitions and then encouraged him to go for his business idea.

He pounded his fist on the steering wheel, angry that he had let even a thread of doubt come into his mind regarding Gracie. Her true character shone in everything she did. She was full of grace, love, and beauty. He loved her. He only hoped that she would give him the chance to say those words again.

CHAPTER TWENTY-THREE

GRACIE

The brightest sunrise and the most beautiful flowers and birds couldn't zap Gracie out of her funk. Sadness lingered in every step she took as she finished packing her bags. She rolled her red suitcase with white polka dots out to the car and loaded it in the front seat. The larger suitcase went in the trunk. Even that action made her want to cry, because she remembered how Pika had recognized the Minnie Mouse suitcase and asked her about it.

Her flight left at seven, but she didn't want to chance rush-hour traffic messing with her plans. She had everything ready to go so that she could leave by two-thirty. Plenty of time to return her rental car and get through security at the airport.

Lexi had tried again to get her to contact Pika, but

Gracie refused. She needed space. Time would help her learn what had really happened to Pika and her heart.

"At least call him before you leave," Lexi begged. "He really loves you, Gracie."

"I'll call him when I land in New York."

Lexi sighed. "Okay, be stubborn and take your broken heart with you even though you don't have to."

Gracie smiled. "Everything will work out the way it's supposed to."

As she pulled away from the bungalow that she had worked so hard to redecorate, she hoped that her words were true, because at that moment, she didn't believe them.

The highway to Lihue was slow-moving, and Gracie had the unfortunate luck to get behind a beat-up pickup packed to the hilt with furniture. With every curve of the road, the couch on the very top would sway and Gracie would hold her breath. A few more miles and she should be able to get around them, she kept telling herself, but surprisingly, the mountain of furniture kept picking up speed.

She finally found an opening to pass the pickup and breathed a sigh of relief. She accelerated and started to pull to the left, but at the same time, the couch decided to come loose from the tower of furniture. It bounced off the open tailgate and hit the hood of her car. Gracie screamed and held tight to the steering wheel, braking hard. The couch crashed into her windshield and then flew up over her car. That's when Gracie saw that the pickup had stopped in front of her. Swerving, she careened around the vehicle, hit the cement barricade, and then everything went black.

CHAPTER TWENTY-FOUR

PIKA

It had taken more begging and pleading than Pika had done in his whole lifetime to get Lexi to tell him Gracie's plans. It was almost too late before Derek intervened and told his wife to give up her secrets.

"I'm sorry, but I promised her. She said she needed space," Lexi protested.

"Honey, for being her best friend, you don't know her very well," Derek replied. "She needs Pika. Don't let her leave before she has a chance to figure that out."

"What? She's leaving?" Pika stood and pushed his hands through his hair.

"She got the lead role in the ballet *Swan Lake*. It's the ballet she auditioned for just before she came to the island. They were desperate for her to play the lead because their ballerina was injured." Lexi's face fell. "She's flying out tonight at seven."

Pika looked at his watch. It was almost four o'clock. "If I leave now, maybe I can stop her before the plane flies out."

"Go," Derek said.

Pika raced out and jerked the door open to his pickup. He sped as fast as he could toward Lihue. There was still time to stop her. There had to be.

Traffic wasn't too bad, and Pika thought he was making good time until everything came to a standstill. He swore and craned his neck, trying to see what the holdup might be. On the left side of the road, he saw flashing lights. Pika groaned. The wreck would probably delay him another fifteen minutes. He tried calling Gracie's cell phone again, but there was no answer. At least this time it didn't go straight to voicemail. He'd left her a dozen messages, and something told him that she hadn't listened to any of them. When he'd told her about Leilani and the unexpected kiss, Gracie had run. She'd reacted much stronger than he could've foreseen and blocked Pika from her life. Her fear was guiding her actions instead of her heart. It was the only thing that explained why she wouldn't even talk to him.

He edged closer to the wreckage. There was a car on its side and a pickup with furniture trailing all over the road. Bits and pieces of broken furniture and taillights littered the scene. An ambulance was there, so things should be cleared up soon. Pika was grateful to get past the wreck and speed toward the airport.

By the time he parked and got inside the airport, it was almost six. He scanned the large screens detailing information about the flights. His stomach clenched in anguish when he found the flight he was looking for. In bold letters,

Boarding stood out as if to taunt him. He hung his head. He'd missed her. Pika looked around the airport for a few minutes, hoping against reason that Gracie had changed her mind, but there was no beautiful brunette ballerina pulling a red Minnie Mouse suitcase behind her. It was over.

Sucking in jagged breaths, Pika returned to his pickup and started toward home. It was hard to think straight, but a tiny corner of his heart reminded him that there still could be a chance. It would be more difficult, but he wasn't going to give up on her. Maybe once Gracie left the island, she would be ready to talk to him. And maybe he would be flying to New York City to see her dance.

The sun was setting as he came around the bend near where the accident had been. Cars slowed as people stared at the remains of the wreckage. A tow truck had the car loaded up by then. Pika braked behind an SUV that was only doing forty miles per hour. He was about to honk when he saw a red suitcase with white polka dots on his side of the barricade.

Pika pulled onto the shoulder of the road and slammed on his brakes. Most of the workers were focused on the vehicles. Jumping from the pickup, he ran toward the suitcase and picked it up. It was probably illegal, but Pika had to check that suitcase. A luggage tag hung from the handle, and he fumbled to read the name printed inside. He flipped it over, and his throat tightened with fear. ***Gracie Cardulo***. It was Gracie's suitcase. He looked at the car on the bed of the tow truck. It was a similar sedan to the one Gracie had rented last week after Lexi and Derek had returned home. She had been driving their car up until that point.

"Please no!" Pika cried. He took the suitcase back to his

pickup. There were no more emergency vehicles in sight, so Pika drove through the median and rejoined the traffic heading toward Lihue. Anyone who was injured would be transported there, because it was the nearest hospital. Pika bit his lower lip and tried to keep control. He wanted to explain away Gracie's suitcase, but he had seen the car. The windshield was smashed, with not much left of it and there was a hole big enough for a suitcase or a person to have gone through.

CHAPTER TWENTY-FIVE

PIKA

*P*ika sped into the hospital emergency parking lot and jumped out of his pickup. He ran through the double doors toward the admitting desk. "Please, can you help me?" He gulped in a breath. "My girlfriend, Gracie Cardulo, was in a car accident. I think she's here."

The receptionist was an older, heavyset woman, and she offered him a kind smile. "Let me see. Can you spell her last name?"

Pika's voice wobbled as he spelled Gracie's last name. "It's Gracie. Gracie Cardulo."

The woman clicked a few keys and pursed her lips together as she read the screen. "Yes, she came by ambulance and was admitted. You may go back to the nurses' station, and they will show you to her room." She motioned down the hall. "There and to your right."

Pika wanted to ask if Gracie was okay or if she was injured, but he realized that this woman at the front desk wouldn't be able to answer those questions. "Thank you," he said, and he headed in the direction she had pointed out.

He found the nurses' station and managed to keep his voice calm as he repeated the information, spelling Gracie's last name again.

"Oh, sure. She's here," a nurse with red hair answered. "And she'll be just fine. A little bruised, but she's okay. Come with me."

"Thank goodness," Pika said. He followed the nurse to a large room with hanging curtains to partition off the spaces.

The nurse checked behind one and held her hand up for Pika to stay put. "Your boyfriend is here to see you. He's mighty worried about you. Would you like to see him?"

Pika didn't hear an answer, and for a moment, his gut tightened with dread. What if Gracie was hurt and still didn't want to see him? There was no way that he could walk out of this hospital without making sure she was okay.

The nurse leaned her head back. "She said you can come on back."

Pika nearly leapt forward in his eagerness. "Thank you." He walked carefully past the nurse to the other side of the curtain. "Gracie?" he whispered. His heart jolted when he saw her lying on the hospital bed, a bruise on the side of her head.

Her eyes were open, and she looked at him. One side of her mouth lifted. "Pika. How did you find me?"

Pika stepped forward and carefully lifted her hand. "It was your suitcase. I saw the red and white polka dots, and I don't think I've breathed right since. Are you hurt bad?"

She exhaled softly. "Mostly bruised. I had my seat belt on. Possible whiplash, and my head hurts. The nurse was just trying to figure out how to contact someone because I lost my phone in the wreck and I couldn't remember Lexi's number."

"I can take you home." Pika touched her arm, his fingertips like a hesitant breath. "If you'll let me."

"That would be nice. You came at just the right time."

"Did I, though? It's killing me that you were ready to leave the island without even speaking to me." He placed his other hand on his heart. "It hurts something fierce right here to know you think so little of me."

She covered his hand with hers. "I was scared."

"Gracie, I've been so afraid. I can't lose you. I love you so much. I had nothing to do with that fake kiss from Leilani. She let herself into my house and launched herself at me." Pika frowned. "She tried to ruin everything with one stupid kiss. I told her that I would call the police if she ever came back."

Gracie pulled her bottom lip in and watched him carefully, weighing his words. She closed her eyes, and tears leaked out the corners. "I'm sorry," she whimpered.

"Shh, don't cry. I promise I would never hurt you. You have my heart, and there's nothing I can do about it. If you leave, I will be an empty shell," Pika said.

"Help me up," Gracie said.

Pika put his arm around her and carefully guided her to a sitting position. "How's that?"

She nodded. "Better. The nurse said I need to make sure I'm not dizzy." She gripped his arm and leaned her head against his chest. "I don't know what to think. I want to believe you, but I'm afraid."

"Then be afraid. I can work with that, but don't run. If you run, I can't catch you and hold you and tell you how much I love you." Pika put his arms around her and held her in a gentle embrace.

Gracie sniffed and wiped a tear from her cheek. "I have an offer to play the lead role in *Swan Lake* in New York City. I was on my way to audition to make it official."

Pika lowered his head to meet her eyes. "Is that what you really want? If it is, I'll support you. But if it's just a convenient way to run from scary things, then let me give you courage to stay and face your future."

She tipped her face upwards. "Since when did you become so eloquent?"

Pika shook his head. "Since I thought my girlfriend died and took my heart with her. I'm here, touching you, holding you, and I can't think of anything else I want in this world."

Gracie smiled and leaned her head against his chest. "Thank you."

The nurse returned and explained what she knew of the accident and the impact on Gracie's health. "She needs to be monitored for symptoms of concussion. If she develops any other symptoms, don't hesitate to see a doctor."

With Pika's help, Gracie was released to his care. She hadn't answered him when he'd asked if ballet was what she wanted. He worried what her answer might be and mentally prepared himself for that choice. He would support her if that was her desire, and he would pray with everything in his being for a chance to be with her again. He was already praying that her choice would be to remain in Kauai with him.

He helped her to his pickup and flinched when he noticed how dirty it was. "I'm sorry I don't have a more comfortable ride for you."

"This is fine. I'm glad to be out of that hospital with all the noise and beeps." She leaned her head against the seat.

"I brought your suitcase with me." Pika motioned behind his seat.

Gracie smiled but didn't turn her head. "Thank you so much. My pointe shoes are in there with all of my ballet clothing. I always take it as a carry-on in case my luggage were to get lost on the flight."

"It really is a miracle that I saw it at all. The sun was on its way down, and your suitcase was on the other side of the barricade. It must have flipped over from the force of the wreck." Pika drove carefully toward the site of the accident, extra cautious of the traffic.

"I think I'd better pay attention to what God is trying to tell me," Gracie said quietly.

"Oh?" Pika glanced at her.

Her smile was tired, but it was there. "Yes. Apparently, He doesn't want me to leave this island."

Pika grinned. "He's not the only one."

CHAPTER TWENTY-SIX

GRACIE

Gracie closed her eyes. Even though she'd joked about not leaving the island, she still wasn't sure that she could stay. Everything was too jumbled up to think straight at the moment. Her heart had been through a lot, and now her body felt battered as well. She decided not to worry about it right then. There would be time to make those decisions later.

Gracie stayed with Lexi and Derek so they could monitor her symptoms and help her rest. She slept for most of the next day, and when she felt well enough to sit in the living room, Lexi chatted with her about Leilani's devious plans.

"I still can't believe that she would go to such lengths to tear Pika and me apart," Gracie said. She had told Pika and Lexi about meeting Leilani in the market on Monday.

"Pika was about ready to pull his hair out," Lexi said.

"And maybe Leilani's too. I'm so sorry for the hurt it caused you. Do you feel better about him now?"

Gracie wriggled her toes in the soft rug at her feet. "I feel kind of embarrassed and unsure of myself. I feel sad that I hurt Pika by jumping to the worst conclusion."

"It's understandable, given the situation."

"I know, but I wish that I would have given him a chance to explain instead of running scared." Gracie had seen the pain in Pika's eyes at the hospital, and she never wanted to be responsible for that hurt again.

"None of us would ever choose the hurtful experiences, but those are the ones that often define us. Or at least help us see what we really want to do in life. Hasn't this given you clarity regarding your future?"

"Yep. I'll never try to leave the island again," Gracie joked, and then she sobered. "It gave me time to really think about the opportunities I had in front of me. Dance was a beautiful temptation, but I realized that in order to be truly happy, I have to be willing to close that door. Always longing for something that is out of reach won't make me happy."

"Well said." Lexi leaned forward. "But I don't think you have to close that door completely. There must be a way for you to keep that part of your life alive."

Gracie shrugged. "Honestly, I'm still trying to figure things out. I have loved it here, but it might not be the best place for my future."

"What about Pika?"

Gracie bit her lip. "I don't want to hurt him. What if things don't work out with us? What if I'm lost without dance? I need to think about what is best for both of us."

"I have an idea what that is, but I won't push you." Lexi hugged Gracie. "You're my best friend, and you're extremely talented. You can do anything you set your mind to. I hope you know that."

"Thank you," Gracie murmured. She wanted to believe Lexi—that she could do anything—but the fear was there, threatening her happiness. There were so many unknowns that life felt a little overwhelming at the moment. She leaned back on the couch and let out a sigh. Maybe when the bruises healed, things wouldn't look so bleak.

~

A FEW HOURS LATER, Gracie found herself watching the clock. Pika had called and asked if he could stop by after work. It was the push she needed to get up, shower, and then take another nap.

When she woke, she found a colorful bouquet of flowers from her agent, Andrew. She wasn't sure who was more disappointed in her decision not to audition for Odette, but at least Andrew had accepted her choice without argument. She glanced at the clock again. It was after six. Gracie groaned and leaned her head against the couch. She was tired of doing nothing, but she didn't have the energy to do much more.

The doorbell rang, and her heart buzzed with the same excitement that she'd grown accustomed to—how had she thought she could have lived without Pika?

Lexi greeted Pika and brought him into the living room.

"How's my beautiful dancer?" Pika sat next to her on the couch and hugged her gently.

"Not as fragile as you think," Gracie replied. "I have a dull ache in my neck, and I'm sore but feeling better today."

"I'm glad to hear that, because I wanted to ask you on a date."

"That sounds nice." Gracie cuddled up next to him.

"Do you know what Friday is?"

Gracie smiled. "I think so. It's the day you either love or dread, depending on life circumstances."

Pika chuckled. "Yeah, I'm looking forward to it this year. Will you be my Valentine?"

Gracie couldn't help laughing. This side of Pika was charming and cute. "Only if you'll stop treating me like I'm going to die tomorrow."

"Okay." Pika leaned in close and whispered, "If you'll give me a kiss that says you aren't going to leave tomorrow either."

With a smile, she leaned forward and gave him a chaste kiss. "Good?"

Pika growled and nuzzled her neck. "Not nearly, but will you go out with me?"

"I'd like that. What do you have in mind?"

Pika glanced toward the kitchen, where Lexi was chopping vegetables. "Lexi is helping me with something. Don't worry. It'll be low-key."

Gracie needed to talk to him about the way she had acted. It was time to apologize, but her stomach was in knots over the right words to say. "Pika?"

He turned and offered her a brilliant smile. "Yes?" There was so much love in his eyes. She felt even more foolish for how she'd reacted.

"I'm so sorry that I freaked out when you told me about

Leilani kissing you. At the time, I worried that you had let her kiss you, but I know you wouldn't do something like that. I let fear take over my good sense."

"Hey, don't worry. I'm not mad. I understand what you mean. I should have been able to stop her, but she really took me by surprise. I realize how that must have hurt you, and I can't imagine how it must have felt." He put his arm around her and pulled her to his side. "I love you."

Gracie rested her head on his chest. "You too." She wanted to say the words, but part of her held back. If she couldn't make it work on this island, then she didn't want to hurt Pika in the process. She just needed a little more time to figure out what was going on with her heart and her mind.

CHAPTER TWENTY-SEVEN

GRACIE

By Friday, Gracie was feeling much more like herself. She was back at the bungalow, and when she asked Lexi about moving out, her friend insisted that she needed to stay there until Lexi and Derek decided what to do with the house. Knowing those two, they would come up with some plan for her to stay in the home until they bought another home to remodel and redecorate. That thought didn't scare her at all. In fact, it might have even caused a little excitement about a potential future.

She tidied up the rooms and enjoyed the peaceful feeling that was part of the home. Pika had taken another group of tourists out fishing yesterday, and he'd given them surf lessons as well. Today was Valentine's Day, and he had something special planned for her that involved Lexi and Derek. When she had asked Lexi for details, her friend had told her, "Don't spoil his surprise. Just wear one of your sundresses and enjoy yourself."

Gracie listened to the local Hawaiian radio station while she prepared for her date. She chose a dark pink sundress that flowed just above her feet. The casual, yet dressy look, paired with strappy, silver sandals and silver bangle bracelets, gave her the effect she was looking for. She pulled her hair into a loose bun and let a few curls fall around her face.

The doorbell rang about thirty minutes before Pika was supposed to arrive. Gracie panicked because she hadn't finished writing his Valentine card. She hurried to the door and saw Pika's mother, Kima, on the porch. Kima was holding a medium-sized cooler and seemed nervous.

Gracie opened the door and pasted on a smile to hide her own worries. "Hello, Kima. Come on in," Gracie said.

Kima smiled. "I was hoping I would make it here before Pika picked you up."

Gracie's throat tightened. She couldn't handle any more interference from well-meaning women in Pika's life.

"Don't worry. I come in peace." Kima chuckled. She opened the cooler at her side and pulled out a beautiful yellow plumeria lei, which she held toward Gracie. "I made this for you."

Gracie put her hand to her heart. "For me?"

Kima held the lei up. "May I?"

Gracie ducked so that Kima could place it over her head. The scent of the lovely flowers enveloped Gracie, and she smiled. "Thank you so much. This matches my dress perfectly. But I don't understand. What is this for?"

"I know my son loves you. Heaven knows I tried to

interfere, but he knows his own mind." Kima followed Gracie to the living room. "It's you, Gracie. You're the one he wants, but he's afraid."

"Afraid of what?" Gracie looked at the waxy flowers on the lei. Pika was strong. He had no fear that she knew of.

"That he's not the man that can provide for you in the way you need."

Gracie looked down and then lifted her eyes to Kima's. "But I don't need anything. Just him. He knows that."

Kima gave her a gentle smile. "I'm not sure he does. All of Leilani's interference gave him some doubts. I didn't help either, and I hope you'll forgive me for that."

"Of course I forgive you. Pika is your son. It's natural that you want what's best for him," Gracie said.

"See, this is why he needs you. You have so much grace about you. I am so happy that Pika found you."

"Thank you. Your son is a wonderful man," Gracie said quietly.

"Then tell him that. He needs to hear it from you. He's with you now, but he's holding himself back because he thinks he's not worthy of you."

Tears came to Gracie's eyes. She had been hesitant to tell Pika she loved him since her accident. She still felt chagrined when she thought of the crazy mistake she'd almost made to leave Pika behind. It was like they were at the beginning stages of dating all over again, with Pika treading carefully and her heart doing the same. "I love Pika. He is the best man I know. I can't think of anyone who could provide for me better than him, because all I need is his love."

Kima smiled. "Tell him that." She gave Gracie a hug.

"Welcome to the family."

The meaning of Kima's words took her breath away. Gracie nodded. "I'll talk to him." She hugged the woman who could become a permanent part of her future if she continued to step forward with courage. Gracie's heart fluttered with hope. "It's Valentine's, and Pika asked me if I would be his Valentine. I intend to assure him that I'm all his."

Kima's eyes shone with moisture, and her smile widened. "Have a wonderful time."

"Thank you again for this beautiful lei." She let Kima out and hurried back to her bedroom. The simple Valentine she had made for Pika was the best gift she could think of to give him.

Pika arrived early to pick her up. He whistled when Gracie opened the door. "You are the most beautiful woman I've ever seen."

"And you're the most gorgeous guy I've ever seen." He wore a Hawaiian dress shirt printed with maroon flowers and tan slacks with sandals. Outside of church, it was the most dressed up she'd seen him. He was incredibly handsome.

He put his hands on her arms and bent to kiss her, but then he paused when he noticed the lei. "Where did this come from?"

"Your mother gave it to me." Gracie closed the distance between them and kissed Pika before he could speak.

He chuckled and hugged her carefully. "That is some good news. My mom only gives leis to people she loves."

Gracie felt her cheeks warm with a blush. "I'm looking forward to getting to know her better."

Pika beamed. "This day just got a whole lot better." He touched her cheek. "Thank you for being patient with my mom. She really is an incredible person."

"I believe you, because she raised an incredible son." She put her hand over his.

Pika took her hand and nearly bounced down the steps as he led Gracie to his rusty red pickup truck. When he opened the door, Gracie gasped. The interior had been carefully detailed, and although the seats were still beat up, they were polished.

"It's so clean." She turned to Pika. "I'm excited for tonight."

Pika brushed a kiss across her cheek. "Me too."

He didn't drive toward the north shore, and Gracie began to wonder if she might know where he was taking her. A few minutes later, they pulled up in front of the Beach House restaurant, and Gracie smiled. "I bet this place will be busy tonight."

"That's why we're here early," Pika replied. "And don't worry. Lexi and Derek took care of everything. They are going to meet us here since our first reservation was canceled."

"Monday seems like a lifetime ago," Gracie said. "So much has changed since then."

"And yet, it's stayed the same." Pika helped her from the pickup toward the restaurant.

They were seated at a table with a view of the ocean that was breathtaking. "Sunset view," the waiter said. "Lucky couple."

"Thank you," Gracie and Pika said at the same time.

They chatted and placed their orders and enjoyed the

ambience of the restaurant. The area was filling up with couples who looked like they were happy to be together for Valentine's Day.

Gracie looked at Pika with a soft smile and then cleared her throat. "What you were saying earlier about things staying the same ..." Gracie put her hand on Pika's arm. "It's also different, and I want to make sure you know that. I made you a little Valentine. Can I give it to you now?"

"Yes, but I have a little surprise that can't wait." Pika covered her hand with his and squeezed her fingers. "Is it okay if we go outside for a few minutes?"

Gracie glanced outside to where the sun was sinking toward the ocean. "Of course. We don't want to miss the sunset!"

They walked out the back of the restaurant, and as they approached the edge of the patio, Gracie spotted Lexi and Derek. They were smiling brightly, and Lexi held a beautiful potted orchid. The flowers were dark magenta, and there were over a dozen blooming.

"Happy Valentine's Day," Derek said as he stepped forward. "You can call us Mr. and Mrs. Cupid."

Lexi nudged him. "We're not supposed to say anything yet." She held the orchid out to Gracie. "I'll keep holding this, but take a look at how beautiful this plant is. Won't it be perfect in your living room?"

"Yeah, I noticed there was a spot on the end table by the window," Pika said with a wink.

Gracie held the plant and smiled at Pika. "He knows I've been looking for something to put there as an accent piece. This will be perfect." She handed the plant back to Lexi and hugged Pika.

Derek cleared his throat, and Pika stepped back and turned around. Gracie saw a flash of purple pass between the two guys.

Pika laughed and slapped Derek on the back. "Thanks, bro." Pika turned back to her. "I have a special Valentine for you, too." He handed her a lavender card with her name written in all caps.

Gracie felt a little thrill as she opened the card. She hadn't expected anything from Pika; just the fact that they were together was the best Valentine's gift she could have asked for. Her hands shook as she wondered why he needed Lexi and Derek's help. Maybe he didn't want the orchid to be smashed. She pulled out the card and admired the front with sparkly hearts that said, **With love, to my Valentine.**

She opened the card, and a folded piece of card stock slipped out. She read the card first.

You are my sunrise and my sunset. I love you, and I want you to be happy. I hope this helps.

Love,

Pika

Gracie glanced at Pika as she lifted up the letter from inside the card.

He smiled and nodded. "Go ahead and read it."

She unfolded the card stock and immediately noticed a picture of a building with a photoshopped banner above the front doors. *Kauai's Ballet Company in cooperation with Burke's Higher Steps.*

Gracie sucked in a breath and continued reading the flyer, which advertised ballet lessons featuring the highly acclaimed performer Gracie Cardulo.

She looked at Pika and put a hand over her mouth. The flyer listed some of the prestigious dance companies and plays that Gracie had been a part of and described the different classes available. At the bottom of the flyer was a handwritten note.

Gracie,

You are the most important part of my life. I want you to be happy, and I see how hard you've tried to live here without dance. I worked with Lexi to figure out a way for you to have the best of both worlds. You don't have to give up dance forever. It can be a part of your life every day that you want it to be. If you choose, you can live on this beautiful island, teach dance, lead performances, and explore with me. I will do anything for you to be happy. If that means I have to let you go, then I will, but I hope that this dance company could be the thing you've been searching for. The people of Kauai need you, and heaven knows I do. I love you more than I thought was possible.

Love,

Pika

TEARS TRICKLED down her cheeks as she looked up and locked eyes with Pika, Lexi, and Derek. "I don't know what to say. This is so amazing."

"Then say yes," Pika said. "Stay here with me."

"I'd already planned to." She reached out and hugged him tightly and kissed him. A moment later, she crouched down to pull the Valentine from her bag. She handed it to

Pika and wiped her cheeks. The card contained a simple note:

I choose you and Kauai forever. I love you! Gracie

Pika whooped and picked her up, swirling her around. Lexi and Derek cheered, and no one seemed to mind that they were making a scene. The sun was bleeding into the ocean in oranges, pinks, and reds, and it was picture perfect. Derek took a photo of Gracie and Pika standing with the ocean and the brilliant sunset at their backs.

"Happy Valentine's Day," Pika said.

"Happy every day," Gracie replied, wrapping her arms around his neck.

She trailed her fingers through his hair and lifted her face to his. Pika smiled at her, and Gracie softened at the love in his eyes. The feeling between them was powerful, and she felt the love arcing across every nerve of her body. Gracie kissed Pika as the sun melted into the ocean and her heart danced with the possibilities of the future—their future, together.

The End

HAVE you read Lexi's story? Start reading *Hawaiian Masquerade* and discover more about the Burke Billionaire Romances!

If you've already read all of the Burke Billionaire Romances, check out a sneak peek of *How to Fetch a Fiancé*, available in ebook, print, and audio.

Chapter 1

"Fetch!" Audrey called as she threw the Frisbee across the park. Her German Shepherd, Duke, launched after it with a yip. He careened through a copse of trees, making Audrey cringe, but showed up a moment later with the yellow Frisbee in his mouth. She reached for it and Duke pulled back. "Hand it over," Audrey said in her best motherly tone. Duke let go of the Frisbee, his tongue lolling to the side. "Yes! Good boy!" She patted him on the head, happy with his progress. "Keep up these manners, and you'll be ready to play fetch with the girls."

Duke straightened up and looked past her to where Katie and Lizzie, ages nine and six, were swinging and giggling. Audrey watched the girls with a smile. They had adjusted well to Tennessee, although the move had been full of drastic changes: no more Daddy, all new friends, and even a huge climate change from Oregon. It had been almost two years now, and Audrey's stomach still clenched when she thought very long on the life she had before her husband cheated on her. She shook her head and turned back to Duke. "Ready?"

Duke stood at attention, determination in his eyes. Audrey flipped her wrist, sending the bright yellow Frisbee on a somewhat wobbly course through the sky. "Fetch!"

An invisible gust of wind pushed the Frisbee off course, and it veered right toward the sidewalk. Audrey watched in horror as a man in a suit, talking on a cell phone, walked toward the flying disc. Before she could call out a warning, the Frisbee hit him in the side of the head, and Duke barreled into him, chasing after his toy. "Duke, no!"

The man fell on the grass, his cell phone flying behind him. Audrey sprinted toward the man, arriving just as Duke dropped the Frisbee and licked his face. "No, Duke. Off!" Audrey waved him away and crouched over the man lying on his back, his eyes closed. Surely the Frisbee hadn't knocked him out, had it? A red welt rose up on his temple, and Audrey parted his thick brown hair to assess the wound. "That's going to be tender. I'm so sorry."

He grabbed her wrist, wincing. "It already is."

"Oh! You're alive—I mean, conscious?" She put her hand on his chest, surprised at the hard physique that was well covered by his pinstriped suit. Duke hovered next to her, and she elbowed him away to keep her dog from licking the poor man again.

The man chuckled, and then he looked up at her with eyes so brown they were almost black. He touched the side of his head again, his dark eyebrows pulling together. "Stunned, embarrassed, *and* still alive." He sat up, wincing once more.

"I'm so sorry," Audrey said. "The wind came out of nowhere and launched the Frisbee into your head."

The man looked around and held a hand out in the perfectly still air. "What wind?"

Audrey straightened, noticing that there wasn't even a breath of movement. She closed her eyes. Not only had she hit this guy in the head with a Frisbee, now he probably thought she was making up things to excuse her abysmal throwing skills. She shrugged. "It was there. I'll admit I'm not a great aim, since I'm throwing for my dog anyway, but I saw it. Duke was headed one way and the Frisbee veered off—right into the side of your head."

"Well, I'm all right now." The man rolled his shoulders back and stood slowly. Audrey couldn't be sure, but it looked like he was biting the inside of his cheek. He looked at Duke, and his jaw started ticking.

"Please don't blame my dog. Duke has a lot of spirit, but I work with him every day."

He shook his head. "I don't." He turned and scanned the grass until he found his phone. He bent down and picked it up, examining it before sliding it into his suit pocket.

Audrey blew out a breath, relieved that she hadn't caused his phone to break. "Well, again, I'm really sorry."

"Apology accepted. Better work on that aim, though." He winked.

"Hey, I can't control the wind," Audrey protested.

He looked up toward the sky. "I believe you. I'm just wondering what message God was trying to send me with that Frisbee."

Audrey pulled her shoulders back, the familiar tense

knot popping out between her shoulder blades. Her ex-husband, Drew, was an upstanding member of their congregation while he was cheating with the preacher's wife. "God doesn't have anything to do with it. It was an accident. That's all."

The man pulled his gaze from the heavens and back to her face. "I think the man upstairs has a lot more to do with things than we ever give him credit for."

The well of emotions Audrey kept tamped down started simmering beneath her skin. "I'm glad you think so. I need to go check on my girls. If you'll excuse me."

"Okay." He nodded, but continued staring at her. "Have a good day."

"C'mon, Duke." Audrey grabbed the Frisbee and walked as fast as she could toward the swing set. She hadn't found a reason to give the man upstairs credit for anything in the past two years except ruining her life. She could still feel the guy she'd hit staring at her as she approached her girls, but she didn't look back. There was no room in her life for good-looking men who still smiled after being hit in the head by a Frisbee.

***

Troy Jackson stood on the sidewalk for a few seconds more, watching the petite red-haired lady practically sprint toward the swing set with her German Shepherd chasing after her. Those red curls looked burnished in the sunlight, and even though she wasn't facing him, he could still see her clear blue eyes. She'd narrowed them, her expression filled with hurt, just before she'd left.

When she'd touched his head, he'd felt something. He'd

been closed off for so long that it was barely recognizable, but the power coming from her couldn't be ignored. And then her eyes ... She'd left in such a hurry, running from her feelings so fast that he didn't even get her name.

Troy smiled. When the woman had started talking about the wind knocking the Frisbee into his head, he couldn't believe it. Just moments before, he had been on the phone with a businessman wanting him to take on a new client. As owner and CEO of Arise Music, a Christian record company, Troy had to be very selective with the singers he brought in. Every day he prayed and asked God to help him run his business the best way possible. He'd been on the fence about this new singer and was worrying how to make the decision before the Frisbee had hit him, ending the call and helping him make the choice that he had been ignoring all along.

He was about to explain himself to the red-haired woman, but as soon as he started talking about God, the woman had turned stiff and cold and left. Troy was hoping to introduce himself before he inadvertently ended the conversation. He kept thinking about the redhead all the way back to his office on Music Row. The little bungalow where he worked still seemed like a dream come true sometimes. His father had asked him a few months ago, "Why haven't you converted to a high-rise building with all the dollars you have hanging around? Why not go to a nice new office space?"

But Troy loved his office, and he liked staying close to the roots of the business. His company was approachable, and he liked that because he never knew who God would send through his door next. When he reached his office,

Mike Cheatham, the A&R director of Arise, was waiting for him as if he'd scheduled an appointment, which, as usual, he hadn't. Troy hardly had a chance to say hello before Mike launched in on the next task on his agenda.

"Troy, it's past time for making decisions on the new vocal coach for Felicia Perry. Can we please take a chance on this woman I've been researching? She's new to the scene here in Nashville, but I think she can offer something that others we've interviewed haven't so far."

Troy stuck his hands in his pockets and smiled. Mike often put in more hours than Troy, so he did his best to work with Mike's requests, but he'd already gone over this twice. "It's been a rough day, Mike. I just got knocked in the head by a Frisbee trying to walk through the park. I'm wondering what I'm missing here. I told you I don't want to try someone who is untested on a new talent."

Mike paced back and forth across the office. He was in his mid-forties, bald, and had a slight paunch to his belly. He had jowls bordering on bulldog, and that image always stayed in Troy's mind. Mike was a bulldog when it came to the business, and he was good at his job. He turned to face Troy. "Just give her one shot. I can bring her in to work with Felicia so we can see what we think."

As the arts and repertoire director, or A&R director, Mike was assigned to work with every artist at Arise to fine-tune the artist's abilities; that included working with naïve young singers untested on the stage as well as prima donnas (and yes, some men fit that description, too). Felicia was not a prima donna. She was an innocent young girl from Alabama who had grown up on Bible songs and wanted to be part of a Christian band. "You know I don't like messing with these things too much," Troy said. "Felicia's voice is beautiful, crystal clear, and she has a message. We need to help her with some of those wild pitch points, but I don't want somebody telling her she has to have all this soulful stuff to be a Christian singer."

Mike was already nodding. "I know that. I wouldn't approach you with this idea if I wasn't sure that she could do it."

Troy turned and looked out the large picture window of his office. Late May was a beautiful time in Nashville, with mild temperatures and everything looking green and vibrant. Part of him wished he could head out early and go for a drive. Instead, he closed his eyes for a moment and thought about what needed to happen. The right vocal coach had to have special talents to refine the singer's voice, while at the same time not changing it into something that it wasn't.

"Troy, it's a one-time session to see if we like her. Come on." Mike's deep voice had a bit of growl to it.

Troy sighed. He'd hired Mike because he trusted him, and Mike hadn't let him down yet. It was time to put that trust into action again. "Okay, go in and get it scheduled with Rachel. And I'll at least listen."

Mike clapped Troy on the back. "Hey, maybe God was knocking sense into you with that Frisbee." He laughed as he left the office.

Troy sat down at his desk and put his hand to his temple —it was tender to the touch. He immediately thought of the woman from the park. He could still see her red hair catching the sunlight as she walked away. He didn't know what it meant, but hopefully with patience he would find out.

Read the rest of *How to Fetch a Fiancé* available in print, ebook, and audio. Learn more at www.rachellechristensen.com

Makes 2 large smoothies

1 cup water or ice

1 can coconut milk

2–3 large handfuls spinach

*Blend the first three ingredients on smoothie cycle or for about 45 seconds

Add:

1 cup pineapple chunks

¼ cup unsweetened coconut flakes

1 cup frozen strawberries

1 scoop protein powder

1 Tbsp hempseed oil or flaxseed oil

1 Tbsp coconut oil

Blend all ingredients together and enjoy!

ACKNOWLEDGMENTS

I am so grateful to God for helping me through the past few years. I got divorced, and a year later, I broke my back. It took an entire year to recover from the broken back and traumatic surgery. I still haven't regained all of my strength. I was able to finish a couple books, but as I struggled with chronic pain and depression, I wondered if I would ever be able to write another book. There were so many attempts—frustrating stops and starts—and then Covid happened. The pandemic affected everyone, and for my family, it meant that I began homeschooling four of my five children. It also meant that I could say goodbye to any ideas of writing another novel as I poured all of my energies into teaching my children.

Something amazing happened, though, as I worked with my dyslexic son. We discovered new programs that could help him in reading *and math*, something that we'd missed before. And then I discovered that another one of my children also has dyslexia, and I started crying all over again. It seemed that the harder I worked, the further I fell behind.

The sun rose again, and God showed me how I could do the most important things. I stopped worrying about writing and focused everything on figuring out how to help my brilliant children to learn in their own unique way. I discovered that my mother-in-law owned a program specifically for struggling readers, and she began tutoring my kids. We've seen a huge breakthrough there. We are still on the journey, but it is one of wonder and optimism instead of frustration and tears. Once those things fell into their proper place, doors opened up and I was able to finish writing the novel I started two years ago in the space of one month.

This couldn't have happened without my husband. He loves me and he believes in me, and I'm madly in love with him. Thank you, Tyler. My children are a wonderful blessing and yet at times a pretty big trial! I love them so much for what they teach me and their patience with my inadequacies. We have so much fun and laughter in our home because of those five beautiful kids.

I want you to know that I have the best parents in the world—I really do. Mom and Dad, you have been my rock when the earth seemed to fall right out from under me. You have never hesitated to help me, to encourage me, and to lift me so that I could go after my dreams. You are a part of every book I write. I love you so much!

I'm thankful for you, a reader like me who enjoys getting lost in a good book. Thank you for choosing my book. I hope that if you have hard days, you'll remember the good feelings from this book. If you enjoyed this book, would you consider leaving a review at your favorite places or passing this book along? Your support helps me to write the next book. Until the next page, enjoy the sunrise.

Rachelle

Photo by Erin Summerill

Rachelle writes mystery/suspense, clean romance, and women's fiction. She is the mother of a large family and she solves the case of the missing shoe on a daily basis. She enjoys raising chickens, laughing with her family, and traveling with her husband. She graduated cum laude from Utah State University with a degree in psychology and a minor in music.

Rachelle is the award-winning author of over twenty

books, including *The Soldier's Bride (a Kindle Scout Selection)*, the Rone award winner for mystery, *River Whispers, Diamond Rings Are Deadly Things, Hawaiian Masquerade,* and *the Echo Ridge Romance series.* Her novella, "Silver Cascade Secrets," was included in the Rone Award–winning *Timeless Romance Anthology, Fall Collection.*

Join Rachelle's VIP mailing list to learn more about upcoming books and get your free book at www.rachellechristensen.com.

Free Book!

Thrills for the Heart

FOR A LIMITED TIME

Sign up for Rachelle's
VIP Mailing List
to get your *FREE* book.

★ ★ ★ ★ ★

Get started here:
www.rachellechristensen.com